CW01303220

Military
Volume One

A Black Bible Novel Collection

By

Jon Klaar

Table of Contents

Sakura in the Gravity

Audrius Razma

"Only our children will know the truth."

-The Real Man

Sakura in the Gravity

Three friends one night in Japan receive a text message from an unknown number offering money for killing Yakuza; their journey of friendship in a military drama begins.
Their fight for life and friendship does take in a lot of places to champion their enemies they never intended to see or know about and save the world they live in.

Takeshi Castle

When a business dealer does not pay what he owes, the business comes to a stop.
Welcome to the Northern European mind games from the depths of hell in business he was travelling.
The bodyguard escorted him home from Sweden.
The business dealer, he was a very poor reputation company director.
He was looking for very serious security. When he abused a woman and child, he knew the death threats he had were not threats of compiled letters.
The escort to Klaipeda was on a route through Latvia in a rental car to cross the borders to his mansion of sedition and abuse of power to a poor family.
His driver felt worn off from a long journey home, and it was late night they drove past near Nemirseta forest of the NATO Military facility.
When in the back, they broke their headlight.
The vehicles came to a halt exchanging their insurance details, and the business dealer stepped out with his bodyguard.

He squeezed his eyebrows, thinking those fools can escape without paying double to waste his time on a cold late night.
"This will cost you a lot more and you know it".
The first slug made its way in a bad business dealer's face leaves him to die.
Another gun fire round makes its way to the bodyguard's chest. With a hole in his body, he takes a chance for his life in the forest.
Our gunman with his six-shooter let his breath out.
"Why do you always have to get the right thing before the righteousness gets undone?"
He drove off, and it was never his intent to kill besides the target. He took money and pride to see laying corpse waste before his eyes.
.
A little later, two school children are meeting their senior school friend in the cafe opposite the school.
He is now a fresh recruit to Lithuanian police officers.
His name is Simon Says.
He was a well-known rascal of the school. His graduating changed his views and to be the respectful guy in the ministry of justice.
Lord Ignacius and Magnum Mage who are young and open-minded schoolboys are now thrilled to meet their friend that led them through their junior years in their school.
"I know you just joined the police, but did you hear about the homicide? It took place last week, about a few kilometres away from our town."

"We have plenty of rumours, but nothing confirmed yet."
Magnum Mage stirs his tea and takes a sharp look, not taking his gaze off Simon Says sitting in uniform looking at two highschool friends.
"We will see what death will bring."
0.0
The days have gone and years followed within the days to once more for three friends to meet, but far from where they have grown up.
Downtown Osaka is full of bars and cafes overcrowded with a huge number of tourists from all over the world.
It is usual Simon Says has a bit of coffee and with relief of his breath thinking about his friends he speaks.
"If I would not have to run my mouth so far. I would not have to travel so far from home but I am happy to meet all of you again."
Mage leaning on his right arm places three fingers to his cheek bones to think more of Simon.
"I was always interested in other cultures. I never knew I would explore such an amazing culture with my friends. This is a double bonus."
Ignacius lifts his lips to smile and brushes his long beard before he replies.
"I am not that thrilled working here. I am a noodle chef but I was way happy to gain qualification after such failed school exams. You know guys from my experience, such a country we are in pays a lot more but at the end of the day I am left with a bowl of noodles on my table."

“We were a grand country before the Soviet war criminals. They ruined our economy with their military occupation and threatened everyone with their death camps.”
Magnum Mage thought out loud from their school history books theory lessons they thought they knew.
“Simon, how is your life after getting caught for taking bribes and in police prison?”
Simon replies he is working for a private security agency that is built of a failed policeman like him.
“I enjoy once again providing safety to people and placing handcuffs on the wicked ones.”
“I am just working in the farmhouse of my uncle. I cannot see any future besides this work.”
Magnum Mage was not sympathetic answering his question and did not make eye contact just had another drink from his matcha bowl.
^.^
Our three friends walked to the district of the bars in Osaka.
When they thought they had enough drinks.
Ignacius' mobile phone flashes with a message from an unknown number.
The text message was written he has to reply yes or no for an offer of thirty millions of US dollars for a contract.
he replies yes.
Ignacius says looks to his drunk friends,
“I think you cannot believe it, but I said yes to an offer of ten million dollars from an unknown message.”

"You are joking with me."

Simon pours another drink in his mouth.

Mage abstains from further comments. He is looking with them concern at concern.

When a second message appears in Ignacius' phone with instructions of how they should commit the hit to a local businessman.

Ignacius slams his drink to a table, spoiling his clothes with alcohol, finding it hard to speak out loud himself, keeping it long what he waited to speak long ago.

"Fock it I am going for it even to see if it is a joke because I dislike how locals treat me."

Simon cannot control his joy from a joke he thought to be in and found himself amused about his friends together and he felt a revolt he did in school.

"As a former policeman I advise you against your wishes."

Three friends take a walk out onto the narrow footpath leading from Osaka Castle hill holding onto each other.

The Botched Job

A man walks to a video games venue to see a well-dressed man in a tailors suit.

"Kitsuen wa anata o korosu koto ga dekiru koto o shitte imasu ka? (Do you know that smoking can kill you?)"

He offers a foreign man cigarette.

"Sukidesu ka? (Do you like one?)"

Lord Ignacius grins a smile from cheekbone teeth to teeth.

"Kore ga anata no hai o hiki hagasu koto ni chūi shite kudasai(Watch out for this will rip your lungs out).

Ignacius stabs through tailors suit in his heart with a chopstick, kicks him off his cutlery and rolls kicking dead leaving him be with a bag of rubbish.

Our white Mage is taking a walk along the river talking with Simon.

"What we are going to do if they know Karate?"

Simon slides his arm under his black denim jacket to reach the back of his belt.

"I will go like Indiana Jones and waste no time."

They continued the journey along the river to kill and earn their living.

When Mage and Simon approached the backdoor of the games venue, the lights sparked into the night with slugs entering bodies of men in black suits to see these men dying on the concrete floor with Simon holding his handgun.

They choose to carry on walking without waiting for them to die stepping over diseased like they were left there.

"Dude, where you got this gun from?"

Simon Says is looking at his piece of metal twisting in his palm examining and admiring the equipment he did hold in his left arm.

"I think officers are required to carry firearms."

Magnum shook his head and thought they are making a mistake drinking and believed the luck will come their way.

"I do not think you are an officer anymore."

Our heroes continue walking the building part made of offices to see if the path is clear and hoping to see Ignacius waiting for them at the very end of the destination to kill.

"What would you do if you run out of ammunition?"

"Mage, the gun is heavy."

He smacks two guys over their heads while they jumped out of the corner running outside to see what has happened in the entrances on the lower floor.

"Simon, I am confused. Why you did not shoot those two?"

Simon run out of those bullets and knew the handgun handle is a great tool to break car windows in accidents while he was in past patrol duties to see road accidents.

"This mister Smith and miss Wesson is a heavy coupe allowing me with the other end to knock out cold anyone who opposes their marriage."

Simon did make a journey to the top floor a lot shorter with Mage he gets a gun pointed into his forehead while one of the security guards are talking to him, presumably alert about events, he not knew to be true they made their way in breaking past building security that happed on outside.

He is asking them questions Simon and Magnum do not understand a word they are speaking, they chose to show rather tell their tale.

Simon knows what he should do and gives no break to others taking one step forward and twisting both hands backwards with the guard's firearm back at his jaw making his hand fire into his head.

The blood splatters a little onto their heads while the remaining mass of blood and meat is coming out of the victim's head onto a floor while Simon gently places him onto the floor.

Our Mage was looking behind him how he made it happen a lot easier than he thought to take one man's life it was easy for his eyes to see it.

"I think you could have him leave out cold like the other two guys rather than getting on us the blood splatters and cause loud noise in here."

"I got it covered, we are alive so far and let's keep it this way. Let's keep ongoing because I need to get paid."

Ignacius after dealing with a random guy outside the venue walks along with the coin-operated games machines into the backdoor as instructions said but he is feeling happy Simon said they will get the backdoor covered from outside in case it was a trap.

Who knows if the unknown number will pay so much it might be right for him to think he is safe. T

The trio is still drunk and in normal circumstances, they would swing around the place, but from so much adrenaline into the moment they could not care less.

When he got closer to the main corridor leading the aim got a great idea of how he could finish the job and is running perspective of success in his head.

He hears men walking fast, and a gunshot fired near to where he is lurking.

Ignacius picks up a fire extinguisher and prepares to see if he would need it in case his friends are in trouble.

"Mage, I think we need to stop talking because we are like letting them know we are here and we going to hurt them."

"Like we would not have done this already."

Ignacius swings this big canister for fire equipment learning Simon places his face into the wall.

"Guys, it's me!"

Simon lets go of Ignacius twisted wrist tilting his top shoulders in the art deco wall.

"I know, but I still hate when friends are swinging at me very heavy objects."

Mage thinks of silent treatment they should keep it their focus if they like to stay alive.

"Here goes silence treatment in a corridor."

When they walked a few meters further they have reached their eventual destination and while walking they run a thorough course of action.

Ignacius knocks on the door where is written the Kitaro Hiroshima the founder of Hiroshima Innovations and Developments.

Ignacius opens Hiroshima's office door a little wider to let his head out to speak.

"Jinsokuna ranmen no haitatsu (the speedy egg noodles delivery)."

The half-asleep man in the executive's chair opens one of his eyes to see three men in the next few seconds to tie him up to his chair and shut his sock into his mouth.

Ignacius does ask his teams for tips on how they should proceed with the homicide they are hoping to earn their living.

"What to do next?"

Simon's funny ideas did make humour much open he slides his arm in his backpack and takes out paper masks of geisha faces printed on them.

While three of them are wearing their face masks Simon did took leadership explaining the initiative to explain what he learned about contract killing from a professional police officer's career.

"I have a good idea how to let the contractor know about our job well done."

He takes out a mobile phone from Kitaro pocket and turns on YouBube application on the mobile saying to his friends on the quest there is nothing more interesting than watching YouBube live.

He places the footage to show a live media stream, Ignacius pulls out his mince clever inside his backpack of kitchen tools he carries to work and offers the struggling old man his last words.

"I said you will have the egg noodles."

He minces the target's testicles into nothing near to explain what a piece of meat it is, leaving him to bleed while he is on live video, letting our heroes have enough time to run far away as possible from the crime scene they just made for a promised pile of cash.

They hey left and are walking far from the town feeling drunk from alcohol and quite sick because adrenaline has worn off, Mage keeps thinking this will not go well.

.

The epic night of the adventure having their night out is near an end, the boys are heading back to Ignacius apartment to sober up.

But Lord Ignacius eyes are captured to see shy pair of black eyes gazing at him and in a way saying hello to him.

With quick nonverbal communication, they join their hands together.

"Guys, you can head off without me. I think I am getting lucky tonight and I could use my private time."

Once a new couple is in Osaka Love Motel, Ignacius is taking his clothes off to see his lady is making her slow steps and licking her lips without taking her gaze off him.

But Ignacius grabs her arm and turns her around with his force.

She bends over to the table, leaving Ignacius holding her right arm with the blade she is holding.

Ignacius softly whispers like a tickle of the feather.

"Your blade or my stick up your backside because any of them can end up inside there."

He without speaking much to her do opens her up by ripping her stockings apart with the blade from her arm and ramps up himself into her backside.

When the time arrives for them to experience the moment of epic climax like a fresh couple, he cuts open her throat to let all of her blood sprays open all over the bedroom and then he remarks to himself.

"You should shut up your hole because I dislike talk a lot women."

He showers and goes outside to have a good smoke to learn he forgot his lighter.

Simon lights up his smoke not looking at him he says.

"You know this can be a bit of trouble for everybody."

"One or two now do not matter because this one was vicious. Also, I thought you guys have gone to bed by now."

"If you would have given us the keys you could have said that why we are here but otherwise, please keep it down. Ok?"

"This was the best minute in my life and I was hoping to marry her till death takes us apart, but death cannot make me happy."

"They all look dead to me when I look in their eyes."

Mage comments long far on the horizon not looking at his childhood friends expression understanding his thoughts.

"Ignacius, if you would like to find your genuine love then swap your TV channel and maybe then you experience better luck, rather than thinking everything is a video game while we are drunk!"

Our three friends are sobering up in an apartment in Osaka, the city is making a commotion from sounds of emergency services vehicles sirens.

.

The sun is dusk near Japan, and two men are having a romantic affair with their hands on one another on a lovely evening.

One man closes his eye while another man places his tongue in his lover's mouth.

They finish their passionate kiss, then one of them goes down on his knees when another one lowers his pants and licking begins with kissing below.

He stands up from a tasteful mouth full of the passionate flavour in between the two, he unzips his trousers and turns round the strong sailor onto his stomach to show him how he is appreciating it.

^.^

In a post-war orphanage for children is in the north of Hokkaido, they are sheltering children who lost all of their families during the war, two boys were growing uptight as a fist and to find themselves to be the best friends looking into the world back at them to take it back.

One was Nobito and the other was Kitaro, Kitaro was later adopted in Hiroshima family when he was eight years old.

Nobito made his way into the world as he saw it fit.

Kitaro knew nothing but the love for a good street fight show everyone around who is the boss.

He was very brave and upheld his code of conduct while growing quick and strong into the cold post-war world.

.

When Nobito and Kitaro were sitting by the apple tree in Mae prefecture in the gardens of the apple farm. They left to see the farming community on their school trip from the orphanage.

"You know when I see apples on a tree it makes me think."

"What are you thinking about, Nobito?"

"Do all happy people grow up strong and healthy eating apples?"

"I am not sure if there is a happy people."

"I am sure we all can be happy."

"I feel happier already, and I find it funny to talk about it on such a sunny day."

"If you remember we learned from school mythology lessons about folklore from far away places talking about the meaning of apple."

"I cannot remember this lesson."

"Because you never listen."

The mile before he continues genuine-minded expresses his deepest desire to say it vocally expressing he says it.

"Because of apples are said we all must live lives of imperfection because we failed a test and fall far away from our apple tree."

"Does it mean those apples near us on the ground are like us."

Kitaro looks closer at an apple tree and the surrounding grass.

"What is the difference between those apples on the tree itself and the fallen ones."

"I think they are not different at all but the time got them to be a little different but if you think an apple can be on the branch forever it makes us fool for thinking like it."

"I know what are you saying but can it be it's just an appearance and I think any of them can be as good as on the ground or above, it's just a taste that differs from tree to tree itself."

"I agree."

0.0

Within, Kyoto somewhere on a sunny day a young man was enjoying the sunny afternoon all by him thinking how his time had gone by and how half-empty the time was.

It was late summer, but this time the weather was better than ever and he was getting ready to leave because his train back home is going to leave without him.

He was walking mindless and over-thinking, looking into the path where he is walking rather than around him. He accidentally walks into a girl with the impact makes both fall over.

Kitaro looks up and sees a girl who stumbled backwards, holding an empty fruit basket because he made her fall with all the fruits scattering around them.

He apologized and asked her name because he felt wrong for being so dumb.

"I am sorry for not seeing where I am walking because I am a little busy."

Her reply did make a choice the day they meet to find one another seeking a simple life they live to start learning it was never so simple.

"It is ok because I was so in a hurry to be back home I was careless. I am sorry too."

"Let me help you place those lost fruits back in the basket."

He was picking apples from the ground, Kitaro asked what is her name?

"My name is Sakura."

"My name is Kitaro."

He made it clear with a simple smile.

0.o

It was a day full of rain, a woman was walking in the Tokyo hotel district to meet the genuine passion and love of her life.

A little late lovers were finishing up their love affair, to hear a knock on their hotel suite door.

She opens the door to say she is a little busy, the handgun shell drops onto the floor making her fall backwards.

A man who was with her, while smoking his cigarette in the room's corner, says to the contract killer outside the door.

"I hope you do not think I pay you to make me drag her body into the bath?"

"No."

He closes the door behind him and takes dead Sakura by her legs, pulling her into the bathroom.

^.^

Our guys decide once they sober up to forget the night before they head out before a morning flight to shake off the stress.

The money did not arrive and no more messages about it.

"It's a great idea to go out for one more night together to a nightclub because I have work in the morning and I might not sleep well tonight knowing what we have done last night."

"Let's rock on tonight without a fail."

"I know one classy place for Osaka."

They come in a front night club on the front door written Royal Gigolos Nightlife and before they enter the nightclub Mage sends a text message to his grandad written 'EVERYTHING IS OK I AM COMING BACK HOME'.

When they enter the dance gallery on a massive marvel floor, the house music is playing and delayed flashlights are on the floor.

The DJ presents over the microphone about tonight playing DJ Benas Benosis, in the background starting the song, "when the truth comes out and all the joy dies, do you need somebody to love".

Mage looks around and says to his friends he is heading off to the bathroom have been holding it for a while.

Simon takes his drink from a glass bar looking around a marble floor night goes enjoying and dancing the night.

"Do not stay too long because it's my favourite remix playing now and I feel like going out for a dance."

While remixing "somebody in love" DJ is playing and disco flash is on the susceptible friends ordering their drinks and talking to each other the stranger slowly let his blade out of his sleeve and is walking up to them just to get his neck broken from behind to slide on a sofa.

The trouble does not stop there and there is further a man sitting by the table aiming the handgun with suspender just to receive ice pick into his ears and to lie down softly his head on his table.

When Mage comes out of the toilet and says to Ignacius he apologizes he took so long because the toilet was so messy.

The lights come on in the nightclub when the server screams she realises the blood is all over the table and the handgun is on the floor.

The lights come on, music shuts off and all the guests run for their lives out of the club.

Simon standing outside says to Ignacius it is a nightmare on an elm street did found its way inside the venue.

"It has never happened before, but I am sure they need to get some decent security outside the front door because it must be some kind of a psycho job in there."

Lord Ignacius replies clenching his fists irritated antagonizing way seeing his last night ruined with his childhood friends leaving far away home.

Mage does ask they start walking away because of coincidence it was a terrible mistake to stay around before they are noticed within crowds of witnesses near a murder scene.

"Let's keep on walking because we might get negative attention in particular after last night's heavy drinking."

Trio after a few more beers are walking closer to a central station to say goodbye to each other before they apart different ways once again, they think about getting a quick snack from the petrol station.

At the petrol station when they finish their snacks, Ignacius says he needs to use a toilet.

"I head off to the toilet; I hope it's not nasty as our previous place with all of those psycho killers inside."

He blinks at his friends and they return a smile.

Ignacius is using his loo, the man walks up to him and says something to him in Japanese.

Ignacius replies in his native language he is sorry he does not understand. But the man in the cleaners outfit grabs Ignacius on his collar and smacks him on the tiles, making him lose his consciousness. He drags Ignacius into the boot of the black car and then walks off.

Simon felt like he needs a toilet as well and walks towards the toilets when the black car passes him without stopping. When he walks into a restroom, he realises the blood marks on the floor and remembers the black car quickly leaving the petrol station.

Simon runs out when he comes to a situation to understand his childhood friend was abducted.

Mage walks up to him and says did Ignacius just pass out once again on his toilet seat.

"I have no time for this."

He rushes to the first vehicle left unattended and takes it to chase after the kidnappers.

Mage is looking at how Simon drives off with a passenger's van written on it "Korean Cheer Leaders" and is thinking to himself something is not adding up in here.

Simon is in such a hurry he does not notice the situation, he is driving a van full of fashion models who screamed while he is behind the wheel tackling in high speed the Kansai region tight bend roads to catch to another vehicle who have left about 8 minutes ago ahead of him.

The models scream and cry inside their van while Simon is steering the road; he plays the radio for a time being he would not take his sight off the road.

The radio is playing an Asian song in English, "Danger, oh my danger you're in a danger."

The girls in Simons van had enough and started vomiting, also releasing diarrhoea.

"I do like this tune." He increases volume and pulls all the windows open in the van.

He catches up to the vehicle of suspects, drives next to it and flashes his van headlights at them when waving them down with his hand.

Both vehicles come to a halt and the men step out of the black car for Simon to see them taking out of the back of the car crowbars and starting walking up to him.

"Great, what I should do in this shit right now."

The men stop walking up to a Simon in few meters away to listen to the humming noise coming in their direction on a side road.

Out in the forest under cover of darkness drives out a farm tractor driving all over them and not stopping heading back into the dark forest.

Simon looks at what he is seeing and what is left out of those big gangsters with crowbars thinking to himself.

"I am lucky enough I did not step out of this van."

Simon quickly runs up to the black car to make sure he chased the right vehicle to find his missing friend. When opens the boot of the car he sees Ignacius all in tapes and half-conscious.

Simon takes the tape off Ignacius's mouth and speaks to him to check his awareness and condition he is in.

" I came here in a hurry once I met all those hot models but do not go in a van yet to greet them because it's kind of awful smell ."

The Mage walks out of the dark forest and starts helping Simon to pull Ignacius out of the vehicle.

"What is next?"

"We need to drive quicker out of here because we have here the road of dead bodies."

"Apologies, I did not come back with the tractor because it took me a while to learn to use the breaks."

"Tell me about it."

"It was written in hiragana. I do not read Japanese."

"Great it was not written in katakana."

"I would prefer in Lithuanian."

"How about Eskimo?"

"What are you guys talking about."

They help him out of those silver duck tapes set his body free and off the boot to see him find it hard standing on his feet they help him sit on the edge of the boot looking at him in the eyes checking his vitals and observing him taking his breath finding his mind back to their normality they are found themselves in.

The trio boards a kidnapper's vehicle and starts driving anywhere they think can be better and further away as possible.

Fock Me Now Fujiyama

In the Kabuchi Strip club in Tokyo, two women are thinking about what customers are talking about when one replies she does not need to know but they need to keep their moneymakers moving.

Ignacius has a lap dance while is talking with Simon thinking about Hiroshima boss?

"Simon, I think if he is alive, I am sure he is a stand-up comedian by now."

Magnum sitting next to them is drinking water and thinking about the situation getting worse for them.

His friends are inside a strip club, the Bank of Hokkaido makes an international transfer to Orphanage in Siberia to the manager of the charity, Boris Blet.

He becomes curious about the transaction and makes a call to his secretary.

"Do you know why such a huge transfer was donated to us?"

"I am not, in particular, to know about this irregular transaction, but I can see they made before it."

"You can stop there, I will inquire myself from now on."

Three men done with their adventure in a strip club broke in a ramen shop above an old bicycle repair store and are whispering to each other.

"Lord Ignacius, it's not like we are stealing porn tapes."

Simon is helping Ignacius holding a flashlight for him to see what is inside a locker.

"Simon, I am not the one who will fill in a report about three armed thieves from upstairs who were heard laughing and used astral projection to transform into goats."

"Well, in here they can arrest only once."

Magnum standing in a dark corner is thinking how he could see their plan take further steps to avoid further criminal charges besides contract to kill, countless homicides and possession of firearms outside the burglary they are in process.

"Maybe we just leave a cardboard cutout of mister universe pointing out the window?"

But when Ignacius looks back he spoke in a light demeanour he would be sure they can be caught because they made so far leaving a trace of smoking gun they might end up dead before they reach the police station.

"Nope. We will later post them the photocopy of his bottom with a return label on it."

They felt amused and made no further talks laughing holding on their rib cages not to split from laughter vocal points out their lungs.

The next morning Simon was thinking why they had to go through all the problems to break into Ignacius the last workplace just to retrieve the blind man's walking stick.

"I wonder how big is Fujiyama?"

Ignacius opens his eyes because he was falling asleep.

"I think the hill is ok but I know a good place to stay with all the view you can manage from there."

When they reached the Fujiyama Prep School, two out of one was not even thinking about what they are going to do there.

"Home sweet home."

"Ignacius, are you serious?"

He is looking at the torn old rusty fence and the building looks like they abandoned it before they were born.

The green scenery made it look the nature took it back its place covering in and out in green leaves the branches of a plant coming out the broken windows and surrounding eastern side.

"I can feel a bad vibe coming from this house of terrors."

Their friend Magnum Mage made an observation, nearly walking over a bent school fence to see the building a little closer in the eye.

Ignacius jumps over the torn fence and turns back.

"Come on guys, I already posted our postcard to Hiroshima corporation!"

Then he turns to his school friends and walks closer to an abandoned building full of construction hazards.

A little later into the night Ignacius is taking the first watch in case they will become ambushed and Simon with Magnum is talking, looking into the night sky covered with stars.

"Simon, I heard stories they leave such buildings behind because they are full of evil spirits."

He is holding his breath in to avoid making too much noise when Mage smiles and turns his look to Simon.

"I wonder what kind of spook we find here?"

But when Simon replies the sound comes from above, like someone is in pain but very faint. However, Ignacius comes rushing in and holding his breath.

"Boys, I think we are coming outside because it's only one car just parked outside our school."

Trio friends go outside to meet their late hour visitors, they confront them and Magnum takes out his notepad and places it into his right palm before he tackles knife attack into his hardback notepad, retrieving the blade and stabbing the guy through his left palm blocking the knife go into his face.

Simon takes a large piece of wood and smashes it across the attacker's face, making him collapse, and a piece of wood goes into the guy's eye who was stabbed in the arm by Magnum.

Ignacius makes his run into the building, being followed by two men who are a lot larger than him. He runs up the stairs into the room he kept his night-watch and picks up the walking stick they had to break into his former job to take it back; he pulls the top of the wooden stick and now is holding a large silver blade. Then he circles two large guys who just run up the stairs and are losing their breaths making a large slash across one of them in the back and going for another floor hoping he will manage somehow. But when the guy comes up another floor level, he grabs Ignacius arm and gets hold of his making Ignacius arm break and let go of his weapon.

He takes his breath and with a second move, he uses the other hand to make Ignacius lose oxygen, slowly losing his strength. When suddenly comes a low voice from behind addresses the man who is about to take Ignacius life.

"Brother, what do you think you're doing?"

The man is at least two meters tall and wide shoulders built; peeking at them in the dark, making it hard to recognize his face. The strangler quickly turns around to throw damaged Ignacius body to the ground before he makes his run towards the man in the dark who interrupted him to kill Ignacius. The man in the dark does not flinch before he delivers a sudden blow to the killer, taking him by surprise and making him unable to talk or walk with half of his ribcage fractured in pieces. Ignacius takes his last look at the dark corner of the corridor.

"Why?"

But the man walks away yawning.

"I am Jack."

Magnum and Simon find their friend on the floor, they take the car left outside and head out of the area, realizing the plan they had was a pivot point of madness. When van from other sharp turn left flips them sideways on the road.

.

Our friends are held captive inside the factory on the outskirts of Fukushima, the ice-cold water wakes them up chained to the floor in a shower.

Ignacius is feeling the pain of his broken arm and makes a scream from the pain of his broken arm in a chain.

Simon just takes a slow deep breath and says nothing when Mage opens his eyes, unable to see much yet from the heavy hit on his side of the car. "I think we might be done."

After a while, they unchain Mage from the heavy cuffs and take him across to another room behind the steel door. There is standing Boris and Kano looking on badly injured Mage's body and Boris says.

"This one focker is giving you a bad time and makes me a lot richer."

Kano smiles, lowers his face close to Mage and blows smoke of his cigarette right into Mage.

"I think I love them all since they saved us all a lot of trouble, he might be now my best friend."

He places his foot into Mages face, pressing harder and harder his skull against a concrete wall.

"Maybe you will be good enough to clean my shoes?" His laughing Boris reveals the truth behind their master plan.

"Well, I took care of your loose mother when you was focking her and now these idiots just smashed your dad balls because he was gay."

Our Mage uses his neck to push the sole. "What the fock?"

"Oh, you would like to know before you meet his daddy and mummy up above?"

Kano, "I would prefer not to embarrass myself to this shat eater, but I might let you have your fun Boris before I will make it quick. I give you ten minutes to find everything about them from this loser and finish it!"

They brought back Mage to the shower room to see his friends and placed him on his knees in front of Kano and Boris to see how they will react in a group because no matter how much they kicked Mage on a floor, he just was swearing and screaming.

Boris tells them to lower their heads and Kano asks his henchmen to leave the shower room beside Boris.

But Magnum looks with his swollen eyes to his classmates. "Do you remember when we were in school and we're watching the basketball games; we then were cheering from the tribunes above. We were making noise for our class in a game. We will rock you?"

Simon replies tilting his gaze to a side thinking it is the end letting vibrating reply out his frail chest.

"Sure, I was there too because it was a good way to skip lessons."

Magnum hits the hard floor with his knee twice and once with his shoulder into the wall but the Boris kicks him over into a corner.

"This one looks like he likes funny things! Should we shoot this kid right now or do you prefer to play a little longer?"

Kano rolls his eyes. "I do not care about those troublemakers, just kill them!"

Outside factory entrance stops a white van and inside a radio makes beeping sound followed by a man's voice ordering to all special preparation soldiers go to their work now.

The doors open outside the entrance to see who had parked outside their factory, a stun grenade falls the front door under the feet of Yakuzas, about to have a smoke. The live-fire opens from assault rifles pointing out the vehicle killing Yakuzas then three men step by step walks forward opening fire on their targets, wearing the flag jackets they shoot targets one by one.

Magnum smiles to himself on the floor and whispers three words. "Tik Tik Tok, we will rock you."

Boris turns his face towards the exit. "What a heck in a mother of god is these bulls noise coming from."

Kano takes his sixshooter from under his belt and aims to press the hammer at Magnum. "You die scum bag right now!"

However, the venture to pull the trigger was, Kano suddenly notices Boris dropping the floor with bleeding from his chest and forehead, Kano feels faint making him fall too with his body collapsing. His vision blurred dark with his body cold and numb.

The henchman suddenly enters to see his boss lifeless body on the floor and feel a sudden sharp pain in his neck when a knife from the back of his neck pierces his temple open and then turns to the side when it leaves his neck. He drops dead.

Outsider shows a hand gesture to follow him. Mage takes lead to follow the unknown male in black clothes holding CAR15 and P99.

Everyone is busy pointing their firearms in front of the factory, one guy is leading a rescue mission; firing rounds from the other side of the factory, closing the fire circle and killing all armed men, until he reaches his teammates and places hostages inside their transport.

The van is heading to an unknown destination and a driver is laughing and making jokes about how another guy picks a short straw to have hiked over the hills in full combat gear.

Simon felt uncomfortable about the rescue mission and made his mouth to talk in a black cotton bag.

"Who the fock are you guys?"

The Black Commando unit soldier is holding Simon smacks him over the head with his knee, leaving him to bleed from his nose.

But a driver stops laughing. "Come on, we should not treat our guests like this." With their van with our friends, above them is in air NATO, SS Spartacus cargo airship got intercepted by the Japanese ground control.

Their air defence ground operator made a signal to reach the incoming airship.

"This is Japanese military air space asking to identify yourself."

SS Spartacus made a brief reply to have one in return before it let its wheels out in preparation to land.

"This is Scandinavia 101, the strangers in the night."

"We have now the ground lights on, you are safe to land."

A little later and NATO SS Spartacus is refuelling when the van drives to Fukushima military air force gates without making a stop at the checkpoint they carry on driving into the back of a military cargo aeroplane and the Nato SS Spartacus takes off into the night.

Bags come off inside the van to the lucky trio who had a lot to go through. Then from a corner in the van comes a strong smoke, and a voice speaks to them.

"Hello, my name is Mark and be thankful to NATO Commando just saved your stupid heads in this shat hole."

"I would rather like to ask you why we here?"

"Lord Ignacius because I had officer's distress signal from NATO's Private Security unit and heard about you guys leaving a trail of smoking guns all over the island. I think you guys are funny and talented murdering psychopaths who would like to work for me since you know about us."

"I think three of us had enough of problems and we would like just to be home to forget all about it."

"Simon, I am Mark Ta and I am Vice General, a pleasure to meet both of you."

Simon takes his look in a light bulb moment to Magnum Mage and looks him in eyes.

"So you were the murderer on the dance floor?"

The Dolls House

Three friends were having their bowl of soup for lunch and thinking about their plans in Bangkok, Don Meung.

The place is an open-air tent with a trail of ants walking across the table into a bowl of sugar. The sunshine is making the sidewalk look all melting and portraying a desert mirage.

The plan was to make it a holiday before their true journey will challenge their friendship.

They were wearing matching shirts and black denim shorts. The black shirts in white palm tree print.

His head felt the sorrow of sweat on his forehead.

"I do not understand when I had to solute a poodle when we landed in Thai airbase."

"Simon, you know after everything we had to go through, I still believe we had to strap on dildos to surprise yakuza in Fujiyama elementary."

"I do not understand what are you guys talking about sometimes." Their Captain Mage did not care to know the details of their past adventures. Magnum Mage looked forward to the bowl of rice and seafood soup. It was sweet as milk.

"Well, I got lucky with brother Jack."

"What was this poodle they framed on gold canvas?" Simon thinks a little longer, making a pause.

"You have a Brother you did not tell us?" Captain Mage kept his finger on the spoon, keeping it twisting in his hand, looking to a lady in the kitchen mixing herbs and vegetables.

"You got me wrong. It was the guy who saved me in the ghost house. He sounded like Australian, therefore I call him brother."

"I see now." Simon pours a little water and thinks a bit about the place he is in, saying to himself why they serve hot soup on a burning hot day, making him drink all this water is driving him crazy.

"Do you guys remember the game plan Mark Ta has told us?" Their captain noticed the soup coming to their table.

"Yep, we need to find a lost kid on one side of the peninsula and bring him home before we all a fried up, we can do what it takes because if we end up dead we go to hell including millions of lost lives with our failure." Simon stretches his fingers together pulling them in one hand out to let his wrists rest.

Lord Ignacius sets his feet forward under the table to relax his shoulders before their meal arrives.

"Kop-Kun-Krap. Is he so stupid to ask us to do it?" Their meal arrives, and Lord Ignacius appreciates it.

"I am not guaranteed, but it is the job they drew us to now." Magnum Mage picks up between his fingers a silver spoon.

The very moment a drunk guy walks in making a scene, he is VIP taking a girl by the hand pulling her down towards the street.

"Ignacius, what are you going to do because of all the troubles on the loose?" Simon asked him, placing in his mouth all the boiled vegetables and white meat in.

"Let's eat first before we go, otherwise we stay empty stomach." Their captain made well in a good hope intended observation, mixing his rice and white meat to set soy sauce flow.

This said Ignacius stands up and pushes his chair in a way of the couple leaving the scene.

The VIP guy is furious at Ignacius and says to him he should leave.

"Mate, you should had mind your own dam business."

"Me sorry me no englesse!"

Lord Ignacius grabs the chair smacking a guy in the head, takes him by his collar, places his neck on the chair's leg and breaks his neck for good.

All the three NATO heroes make a stroll down the street to avoid attention from what just happened, but the girl approached them.

"Sawadee Krap, thank you saved me. My name is Pan Narak."

"You get better focking lost too or otherwise you sleep in a dumpster." Lord Ignacius just saved ran away.

"You should not be so harsh." Magnum slapped his shoulder in a quick snap, Lord Ignacius unable to see a twist of his arm fast than one second in his mind.

"I am sure she is a prostitute or worse because I just lay down her customer and she is looking so friendly looking for another customer." Lord Ignacius scratches his crotch.

"Here is our ride to our beach resort, let's get in before we become a local sensation."

Simon shows them a fist to the air crossing his left arm punching his right fist walking away letting them know he is no fool.

Our heroes in the night meeting point at a bar. They had all afternoon to catch some sun on their skins.

But one guy and he sat at a reserved table next to a palm tree waving to our three friends. He calls himself El Paso."Hi Hibler!"

"A? Do you have problems with us?" Simon takes a seat closer to him.

El Paso relaxes his shoulders in the chair he is sitting in and moves his lips to each ear cheek.

"Guys, after our active fire standard training I have not seen you, rookies!"

"I was happy enough to know it." He orders a waitress to pour a drink in.

Paso does show two fingers in the air and licks his lips. "I heard you guys are going on a top-secret mission to save the world, it's so confidential you cannot share it on Fokbook? "

"You know Facebook is just communist malware but for free?" Simon made a joke-cracking their rib cages and all laughed before they ordered their drinks.

Our diamond formation heroes are enjoying their pineapple juice and rum, smoking the Cuban cigars El Paso had brought them from Cuba.

"This is a proper Cuban missile crisis here I am holding." Simon draws his mind to closer inspection of burning tobacco leaf held three years in before it leaves to customers.

"You never win against communists." Simon's communism joke made their minds rest at ease before they entered the combat project NATO Vice-General assigned.

"I was long before you two working on these projects when I met Magnum, he was a shy kid before we thought him ways of murder, but most creepy enough is he is a still shy kid."

Once El Paso said, making others smile except Mage.

"Tell me about it, today we run into a shy couple with one guy getting all talk a lot with me before he ends up ill." Lord Ignacius scratches his hair.

"You know this makes me think Mage is not a creep here, he accepts what it is with his heavy heart but knowing how you play all happy and cool when you bend all these fools. I think I should double lock my bedroom while you are around." El Paso drops ash of cigar in an ashtray.

"I know and we had to share the same bunk beds while we had prep training?"

Simon exhaled his cigar smoke.

"We are childhood friends and we are in NATO-like one unit."

He makes another smoke to let his dark smoke fumes fill the beach night air fill air.

Our Mage was gazing into the stars before he had another drink and then all left to sleep since they all had plans.

^.^

They had enough drinking and Ignacius ends up in a royal kickboxing stadium taking a fight to amateur winners stadium in the blue corner.

To see suddenly lights go out and come back on with a loud microphone.

"Can you smell what the debt is cooking?"

Then from the podium to run in two guys wearing spandex shorts and spandex masks.

.

The mage had a good last drink to stay at the seashore to see his friends heading out.

Simon makes a call a little later, about Ignacius taking a walk by himself and knowing about the early flight tomorrow morning.

He heads out to the last location he went missing.

They are asking around at the bar they saw him learn he was talking about amateurs fight he was very interested in.

When they head towards the stadium El Paso taps Mage on his shoulder to tell him to look above into a fog light to see Ignacius' face across the other guy.

The voice in a stadium announces the debut of a new fighter, the Cowboy versus the Big Bulldog, to start in the next half an hour.

They look at each other and say together.

"I think we are all in for a fight now."

The commentator shouts it will be a spectacular night watching this fight: Lithuania vs Georgia!

Mage heads to the TV operator's room giving a light knock on the door to hit the cable guy on his face with the same door he opens.

He walks in and pulls the guy's arms in closing doors behind him.

Our Magnum shuts off all communication lines and runs an ID caller block blocking a few kilometres of all mobile lines off to give some time for them to take Ignacius back.

When the lights shut off, Simon and Paso put on the spandex suits and looked at each other.

Simon adjusts his mask.

"I hope we never do this again."

El Paso does show his genuine smile.

"No worries, our love affair is only between us."

The guys run in a stadium waving at the spectators and heading towards the Big Bulldog holding lighters in their hands to increase their fist blow power.

Simon jumps over ropes takes with him a folding chair and gives a good throw at Ignacius, making him fall down the floor already from weak legs after over a limit of alcohol in his blood flow.

El Paso runs up to the Black Bulldog and smacks him over the floor but he pulls back the ropes blocking his face expecting another blow.

Our El sidekicks him a few times into his ribs, causing his ribs to break and fall onto the floor from the pain he has.

He does not stop and picks the Big Bulldog by his legs kicking him into a groin shouting.

"How do you feel now Mr Big Bull?"

Simon helps Ignacius grab Paso on his sides.

"You should stop, have you gone mad, we should leave now!"

Lord Ignacius does pull El Paso from the stadium floor, leaving the big bad Georgian Bull laying for the crowd to see him fail.

Then a commentator's voice appears announcing.

"We all know how we love American wrestling and we brought you this show and a surprise present. Hope you guys have a good night and applause to our lovely foreign actors."

The crowd gives applause, and Mage once he finishes with the announcement shuts off the stadium lights.

A NATO team runs to the street where Mage is waiting outside the emergency exit with a random car he unlocked from his mobile IT device and waves at three guys running out in long coats. "Do you guys expect it to rain tonight?"

Simon takes off his spandex mask.

"Nope. We were at the Royal Wrestling Stadium."

^.^

The morning of a flight on a TV channel in Thai local news the channel Thai BBD is running a news report in English about the Korean industrial revolution to avoid loss of commerce making more robots to handle the manufacturing industry.

When he notices the news headline, Ignacius does look to a TV drinking ice cold water to fix his health.

"It would be weird to see the machines go on low oil strike and turn the streets like in genesis movies, protesting with blasters against police officers."

Simon walks by to a showroom. "I would not go to work then."

Mage pays no attention to the media on TV.

"The world is changing and those who probably cannot adopt are on a news channel."

They later are heading to a bus stop for the airport, Ignacius does go across the street from a bus stop saying to wait for him while he buys some water.

He walks on zebra crossing to learn that in Thailand zebra crossing does not allow you to have a right to pass the road first.

The vehicle does not stop on a pedestrian line and Ignacius instead jumps away; he jumps on the front of the vehicle when the vehicle runs away with our hero.

Ignacius smashes open the windshield with the driver's face when he places his arm in through the side window and grabs the driver's collar.

He gives a finishing blow to cave in the window into a vehicle and gives him access to the car.

Our Ignacius gets in while on the road and punches the driver's head until the vehicle turns off the road and flips over.

Ignacius pulls out the driver and continues to kick and punch him.

The car pulls over with Mage and Simon, they whistle Ignacius and El Paso behind the wheel.

"I thought you guys might use a ride to this flight?"

The tall guy who was watching the road rage is looking at those assailants driving off and making a smile with waving hands while they drive by him.

A Thai girl walks up to him and kisses him on the check.

"How are you today, Ban Toya?"

Toya looks at her.

"Blat, you won't believe what I just witnessed, Pan Narak."

.

The Mage is sitting in an A16 seat on his flight to Seoul and takes his travel sickness pill to help him have some sleep after a long night.

His eyes are closing, he watches how Simon and Ignacius are already asleep.

Mage suddenly wakes up to the feeling.

He is in Ignacius' body but he is old and sitting in a wheelchair.

The good-looking nurse takes him into a garden and she is smiling.

She then parks him in front of the flower bed, then she smiles and waves to gardeners.

The men wave back and she walks to them, she hugs one and kisses the other one while she is still holding one's private part.

They all smile and laugh sitting on the bench covered by trees but directly under Ignacius' view, Mage can sense how Ignacius feels angry all boiling inside his body but unable to flinch.

The Japanese nurse spread her leg over one guy's leg, giving him access to his finger to go inside her bottom, while the other one is kissing and touching her bare breasts.

The guy pulls his pants down and starts pressing down on her on the park bench.

Mage suddenly feels gravity and is pulled into a space tunnel to travel in time.

He appears in Simon's body, having his eyes closed and feeling like he is kissing.

The body opens his eyes and he can see Ignacius' mother in front of him and a mirror behind he can see Simon's face.

The space tunnel pulls him out again, making him travel across the space once more.

He is now in his own body but he finds out he is a space pirate and the crew captain too.

He is on a mission to other planets to help his crew find riches. Mage travels into a planet of women where they promise a good life; they feed his men; they bed his men and they feed themselves on his men to find out the woman wants his men's soul to hatch the golden eggs.

Magnum rounds up surviving men and heads down into a cave as their revenge to break the golden eggs cave.

He then feels the ground is shaking and lights turn dark for him to open his eyes to see the plane is preparing for landing and he just woke up from having a dream.

The sunny days are in the past arriving at the passport point.

They handle their passports when they enter the checkpoint and when they had left, the passport officer thought to herself.

"Alfa Scheuffer, Tango Ventura and Bravo Dutch; how are strange these Lithuanian's names?"

^.*

Once the team arrived at the location, they left their bags at accommodation in Gangnam sixth-floor apartment and left for lunch to see how life is here and implement the orientation plans of trace and rescue.

"We are now normal tourists from Bavaria, we always add yayaya or ahh when we speak."

Mage is walking and thinking about their future.

"Ya ya ya."

Simon practises his vocal cords.

Ignacius adds his voice. "Ahh."

Our team was heading to the local cafe for a quick shot of coffee and a sandwich when a stranger was looking at them from a building window across the street.

The cafe staff were in a good mood and one guy behind a till was holding an interest in his customers.

He stayed close and joined the table of theirs to learn about customer service first impressions.

"Hi guys, I hope you speak English. I am Bibi Bit. I am happy you like our cafe place."

Simon does appreciate his cafe.

"I wonder if he intends to sit here long before we leave."

He lifts his finger on a coffee cup looking out the window. He places his arm back on the sofa chair and relaxes his feet.

Mage appreciates the hospitality.

"We could use local guide intel about anything we might now know."

Ignacius sits closer to him.

"We could take on subcontractors too."

Bibi Bit smiles and moves his eyes to his fresh interest.

Simon looks back from looking at the window across the street.

"We have one extra teammate on the way since there are four formations in the guidebook?"

Ignacius drinks from a cup of coffee.

"You do not tell me he is the guy who made us a coffee?"

Mage drinks coffee too. "I think he makes excellent coffee. Let me ask you about the time you complete your work and head out to see the nightlife."

They had a full lunch. The phantom was still looking at them outside his window when Bibi Bit did ask how the meal was.

Simon left an extra tip in Won.

"Ya ya we understand how important it is to the hospitality business to provide excellent customer care and we would love to have your time if you don't mind?"

Bit made a small sudden bow.

"How could I help you?" He sits closer and listens intensely.

Mage does make a proposal asking for help.

"Ahh, we are new here and a little worried about nightlife hidden dangers and we would be happy to ask you to have us to show you around and as an extra job."

Ignacius takes out his envelope of cash.

"How about 500000 won for a three day's tour guide after work, ya?"

Bit smiles and starts thinking he could use a deposit to add for his new rent key money to rent his apartment.

Simon knows they need to start with local criminal gangs to find intel that is free of access to lead points, and he thinks about how he could take the point at the moment.

"How about a local place where we could treat you to serve you soup because it is cold here from our sunny place."

"Maybe I could ask you guys how I could spell your names?"

"I am Vlad Tango, this brown hair guy who doesn't speak much is Algimant Bravo and the guy with beard all over his smile is Pioter Romeo."

Simon gives his hand. "I am happy to know you."

"I am sure you guys are funny ones, I am happy to head out. I close the shop around 8 PM so come before then to have shots on the house before we head out."

Lord Ignacius brushes his beard hair.

Mage thanks and adds his hand too to a formal handshake.

Ignacius adds his hand too, turning into a team shake. He speaks.

"Fighting."

All let go of the handshake, the joy flows through their hearts.

They walk into the street, they know they made the first step to infiltrate the local community to look for a crime organization and find the lead to the hostage location before it is too late.

Their Captain made an important impression his team would never forget.

"I think we are now Littland Organized crime gang taking over the control."

Simon looks at him brushing his bald head.

"Do you think it is ok, how about our boss Jon Gi Sigis, you know he hired us from Japan?"

Ignacius understood Simon's improvisation did help his team.

"We will do well in a murder case from our last kill point."

They all smile to themselves while walking away laughing in their minds and repeating.

"Littland group hehehehe." They knew it was too important to fail.

^.^

They end up in a local food stool singing and overflowing soju shots one after another for Simon to see the group of funny guys in a suit with palm tree shirts telling the old lady off.

He stands up and says to his drunk friends he needs to take a leak. Simon walks around the back of the outdoor toilet to find a brick.

He walks up to a gangster looking guy to hit him over the back of his head with a brick.

Ignacius shows up from the other side walking to hit one with his shoulder.

It happens he slaps the guy over his face, making him hit the ground.

They finish kicking them all over the floor. They feel so bad they let one survivor go when he screams.

"I will take you to court for this."

Simon waves with a smile on his face. "You should tell this to the Littland Group."

They come back from a good fistfight to find Mage and Bit holding onto each other's shoulders pointing fingers at each other and saying to each other. "No, it was not you."

Mage stands up and looks at their teammates asking them how long they had to drink by themselves.

"Did you guys have to sock each other off for so long in a men's bathroom ya?"

"Ahh, you just look like you will not sleep alone tonight." Simon takes a seat back to the stool. He is feeling his feet are killing him.

"You guys start speaking English or this tour guy will go crazy." Bibi Bit points his misguided finger at Simon.

Simon opens an extra bottle of soju.

"Hey Bit, have you heard about the Littland crime group around here because we just had their feathers up."

"I never heard of those pricks, show me them and I beat them to a pulp for scaring our beloved tourists here."

"Ahh, then might I ask you who is the real villain around here in case I might run into them?" Lord Ignacius waves to bring more Soju.

"This Aisel Hasel Goon and his prick Sin On. They are always like on crime scenes and all over the news but never seen in prison."

"Ahh." Simon and Ignacius both pick Mage and Bit to head off to a taxi point to help them home.

Lord Ignacius pays the bill and takes a couple more bottles with him.

^.^

Mage walks into a kitchen to help himself with a cup of water for his headache and sees Bibi Bit laying on the floor.

He looks at Simon. "We are holding our team briefing today because our teammate has just landed and should be in an hour."

"No worries. I just quickly helped him to sober up because I think he will have some wonderful coffee once he shows up at work."

"OK."

"By the way, is it the best they had in a street league here abusing this grandmother for petty cash?"

"I do not know, but why did you guys make them scream like pigs nearly scaring me and our buddy Bit? I had to have a good few drinks together to make me forget about it."

"No worries."

"We should announce our fictional crime boss ASAP, about Jon Gi Sigis and his right-hand arm about Jon Sin. We need strong diversion because lawmakers and law administration units are not aware of our presence and won't until we all turn to ashes."

.

A taxi arrives outside their apartment block for a young lady to walk out with a large grey hat and large brown coat holding silver hand luggage in her hand, making her way to three friends waving.

She stops, lowers her head. "Konnichi-wa, I am Sakura Uto."

Simon stands tall greeting her.

"Well, denim and leather have brought us all together."

Secta

Simon wakes up from hospital bed on the northern side of the peninsula border to see his teammates under oxygen and life support machines overseen by the Korean nurses.

He says to himself I cannot believe the dream.

"It was my late father taking me out of the darkness, his face was covered in scars and he was asking me to wake up."

"I can still hear his voice, wake up my son."

***

But before all chances come to light we can follow our heroes journey.

Before she managed to arrive Simon Says went to a gym center and inside he entered a martial arts dojo for his first free lesson. He changed to black tracksuit bottoms and white t-shirt; he thought good sweat will help him avoid a stronger hangover.

Then he did ask for extra lessons to test his skills further because the group was for beginners. When he was training in private sparring the dojo master hit him in his back with bamboo straw to help him fight further, "attack attack", but he beat them up and bent them over their heads for apology suddenly to learn he broke a straw stick in half and stuffed it on their backsides.

"Banzai!!!"

He was shouting and after he went out for a cigarette leaving his new sensei suffer in the dojo.

He drew on his hand three circles elongating the middle one.

"I think it will be perfect Ikigai to them."

Later he was in police custody while interrogated and was asked what it is, and he replied, "it is my dick I whip you with".

He jabbed the station officer down to the floor and grabbed the running sergeant by his collar to smash his head so hard into the wall his hat fell off.

Now he has them tied down on the floor, he starts kicking them and continues his investigation about the missing kid.

When Simon returns Ignacius asks him.

"How is their strong arm of the law?"

Simon drops his gym bag and before walks away he says, "They are still probably deeply in shat."

***

They welcome her into the Hansun apartment residency they rented for a couple days to complete the mission they were given.

She steps in the lift giving a shy smile to see Simon smiling full cheeks back. Ignacius winks at her and Mage keeps a close eye on her and then exchanges expressions.

They walk in through the apartment door and Simon says to her he will personally show her room so she could settle in as quickly as possible and while she puts the bags down, he would make her cup of black coffee.

When she walks away.

Mage is holding his mobile phone in hand looking at the message he just received.

Simon looks at him while he is boiling the kettle he says, "I would love to have one of those super phones but my budget cannot allow it", Mage "we keep minimal contacts with the boss therefore we keep limited connection devices in our team."

Simon, "What is good online for us to know?"

Mage sits down, closes the phone and leans his head back to close his eyes.

"There is nothing much in our network, it just reported that the BBD Brit secret service has gone missing after he decided to accept murder contract and kill one well known boxer. I think the agent 's name is Edward Hogson."

Simon pours in hot water for coffee to brew and places one cup close to Mage.

"I think I was watching the news the other day and they mention some sort of murder investigation."

Then Mage picks up the cup of coffee and starts walking to the end of the corridor, "I will take her coffee to her to see how she is doing and do not forget our codenames we only use because she has her own we do not know."

Simon, "Roger that and over or out", then he places his legs on the table and has his fifth cup of strong coffee today.

Mage walks up to her bedroom and gives a knock to her door, "Sakura-san it is Algimant-senpai and I am holding your coffee."

She opens her door, "arigato".

She uses her both hands to take coffee from him, "I would like to know where the washroom is because Vlad-senpai was so urgent I would see my bedroom. I was not able to know the apartment well."

He shows her around the penthouse suite apartment then he smiles.

"Apologies we were on low funds to have it with a swimming pool." She smiles too.

When she did have her hot shower, the guys were preparing a strategic team meeting and were completing data analysis of geographic and cultural objectives.

She walks in blue jeans white silk shirt and says she is happy to have the work done together.

"I am happy we can work together and I would like to be debriefed how much we are making progress in our case".

Team captain Mage looks across the living room dining table and says to her she could join a spare seat to join the data analysis.

"We have a belief it is an organised local crime syndicate responsible for kidnapping our target and they are believed to make an attempt to ask a ransom at a later date but we have no time left to conclude therefore we are made to act in such a quick way."

Sakura sits down and looks through Daily Bong newspapers archives the team had received from the data analysis team after their field Intel was complete.

"I see Aisel Hasel Goon and Sin On are the top suspects to be masterminds in the conflict to come."

Simon grabs a bit of his lunch sandwich and once he swallows with a cup of water, he takes another copy of the report they had received and pushes across the table to her.

"I think tonight we can raid their nightclub the Iron Quest to see if we can make vital intel points for us to complete on time."

Ignacius brushes his right arm across his brown beard.

"We are the Littland Organized Crime Group we have portrayed the other night and we should press the overseas mafia's attempts to have the race for control of the country."

Sakura looks to Ignacius, "How we proceed."

Ignacius, "we made clear the fictional crime boss and his henchman identity, for us to conclude Vlad is Jon Gi Sigis and Sin On is just a ghost to cause larger distortion."

Mage concludes the team meeting.

"Great, welcome to the northern European mind games, I hope you will like it."

Sakura stands up and makes a short bow.

"Arigato."

Mage suddenly stops to stand up.

"My apologies, I almost forgot our communication codenames because we use pseudonyms while we work but we will need open channel names. I was instructed to inform you I am Live Wire, Vlad is Torpedo, Pioter is The Streets and Sakura is Wildflower."

***

While the daybreak was near the end and night life slowly creeps in the day, the NBL special delivery courier pulls over the back door to deliver the package addressed to Sin On.

The delivery man walks out the driver seat to open the rear van door looking down at the floor and walks to the intercom to dial the doorbell call.

"I have a special delivery for mister Sin On therefore I would be happy to have him sign the parcel today."

Then couple minutes later you can hear the steps taken leading down from office above the ground floor storage gate when delivery man picks up the metal bar near waste container and breaks down security camera; then man opens quickly the door inside grey gates for Simon to spray in Sin On face.

"I hate bad breath", when man quickly collapses Simon throws in the parcel and pulls in Sin On inside the van to escape.

Mage parked the blue van near the district the team was taken to enjoy nightlife the previous day by their new acquaintance Bibi Bit.

"I think Sakura-san, you had a great strategy for us just to locate the important target rather than causing a mess and waste of time clearing their night club."

Sakura was sitting inside the van with Ignacius and was talking about planning and concluding the post-intel action plan how they could proceed the rescue when radio makes a spark and they can hear Simon.

"The Torpedo has completed it and is now heading towards The streets assembly plan."

When they hear a loud vibrating sound after they start their vehicle.

Simon starts his van in a hurry and when he runs the speeding vehicle down the corner he presses the remote inside his pocket to cause a large explosion from a parcel he threw inside the nightclub back gates.

When he stops in the outskirts of Seoul in an old abandoned road around the corner from the cargo container, he radios through to Mage.

"The Torpedo has delivered a patient to the care home."

Mage opens the door of the shipping container.

"The visiting tour has just started."

They open the van doors and cover his head with a coffee bean bag then they gently lift him out the van holding onto his arms and legs carrying him inside the container to place him onto a chair.

Sakura uses rope around his legs and finishes the knot around his waist.

Simon pulls out a small jab needle and injects it in his neck. Ignacius leans back at the side of the container and looks in the direction the sun is setting down.

"Do you think it will work?"

Simon places the lid back on the needle and takes it back into his pocket.

"I am sure it will work Pioter, do you remember when I passed out during our mountain trek training and the big boss brought me back to life with the same chemical to complete the last 10 kilometres run with 20 kilograms bags over our shoulder?"

When Sin On starts to move his head and increases his breathing.

Mage, without waiting a moment to see how he responds to adrenaline, pulls the bag over Sin

On's head and shows him a picture of their mission target.

"Do you know this kid?"

Sin On opens one eye. "Why should I tell you anything!" Then Simon slaps him over his face. "I think you should learn manners before we make you speak."

Sin On takes a good look at Simon and spits on his shoe after Ignacius walks in. "I think we finished here, I just opened his mobile encryption and synchronised his GPS history data to conclude we are dealing with a kidnapper."

Sakura Uto without taking a second longer pulls out her small silver open and presses it twice open to stab Sin On in the neck.

Simon takes a look at her small clenched fist with a silver pen sticking out of it, "What a nice middle finger she has."

Mage start to take the ropes down and asks his team to help him to carry Sin On out the container.

They walk around the side of the container near a large hole they dig inside the ground, they place the Sin On unconscious on to the ground and Simon pushes him with his foot inside.

"I think you guys were doing a lot of labour while I was driving around the club district.".

Mage takes a shovel and starts to throw the soil back into the pit, Ignacius walks up the pile of rocks piled up right next to the shovel and picks one up.

Mage asks Ignacius to stop with the huge rock in his hand.

"We must wait before he has white foam out his mouth to know the black crab poison is effective."

The moment he says about the poison the moment white foam starts to float out Sin On's mouth but suddenly Ignacius throws the large rock on to his head making blood splatter over the ground.

Simon, "I was hoping you will not make me puke today Pioter".

Ignacius, "I just relieved his pain and misery although I know his nerves had gone numb three seconds after he had it but just in case."

Simon, "I think you have problems Pioter".

Mage, "No complaining and we all start pouring the soil back in."

When they finish with the shovels, they take off the overalls and place them in a bin bag, and then hop in their black SUV.

Mage, "I hope we all are happy with our nature sightseeing today?"

Simon, "Yay it was fun fact."

Sakura, "I named my weapon a little finger."

Simon, "I wonder how about us?"

Ignacius leans back in the leather passenger seat, "I would like to call my knife a War Saber."

Simon, "I know all about your walking stick saber."

He starts to laugh and before he finishes laughing Mage interrupts.

"I would call my handgun Daku, because I like to know I can carry at ease inside my jacket and I like it black."

Simon, "I would never think about naming a dead thing with the name but if you guys talk about the fighting spirit, I could have it named a Whistle."

Mage, "How would you justify it?"

Simon, "I think at the times when we did not have real technology, a police whistle was the only way to announce the crimes."

They start their Black SUV and drive off the bumpy ride across into a clear narrow road leading back to the capital.

When they park back at the Hansun Apartments Mage tells them, he will return the SUV and on the way back he will complete the report back to NATO Vice-Commander about today.

He steps out of his taxi and when walks in the apartment lounge he sits down in the one seat sofa, places his left arm at the wooden arm of the chair and comfortably places his spine in soft black leather.

He opens his mobile screen and sends a message in a dating app X-partner a message to girl.

"I think a lot about you and I made arrangements for us to go out on a date, my work is fine so far and I think I will finish on time for a meeting at the cinema in two days."

Then a message comes back to X-partner, "I am happy to hear from you. I look forward to our lovely evening together."

Then he stands up and walks towards the lift, he opens the lift door with the resident card and walks in pressing the top floor button.

He comes back everyone relaxing on the sofa in silence, with their eyes closed like they would seek meditation relief.

"I never thought you guys are doing group nirvana seeking."

Simon turns his head, "I never did but I just enjoy a moment of silence."

Mage walks into his bedroom and takes a fresh towel before he goes in a hot shower.

When they all had a good shower they were enjoying a cold bottle of water and relaxing in silence inside the living room on a large sofa.

Simon, "I think we know a very great tour operator around here."

The doorbell rings and when Ignacius opens the door Bibi Bit is standing outside smiling.

Ignacius asks him to wait for them to get ready in 30 minutes and they will meet across the street in residential gardens.

Simon walks in his room to look for a blue t-shirt with a grey shiny suit he bought from a street merchants tailor shop in Bangkok.

Mage puts on a grey t-shirt and brown slim linen suit and Ignacius pulls out his suitcase white t-shirt and soft cotton blue suit.

Sakura walks in her bedroom and changes to black silk underwear and bra. She looks for her grey cotton maxi dress, brown sandals and takes her black evening bag she is holding inside black pouch, her folding mobile, the top designer watch 'travel machine' and her flower scent perfume she sprays two times around her before she takes white band to place her hair together.

She takes a look in a mirror and is thinking she is cute already to go out with new friends.

When they close the apartment and take the elevator to the ground entrance into the hall Simon offers to give her his arm so she could feel comfortable walking out.

They walk through the lounge of the entrance with brown sofa chairs and silver marble floor through the facade of exotic flowers and through a glass entrance into the path leading across the car park in residential gardens.

Legal Notice

It's an art of fiction never intended to be a resemblance of living but create an alternative reality parallel to our lives, helping us experience a sensation and entertainment of non-existing events.

If the coincidental information about fictitious forms of work comes into mind, they never intended it to mention neither living nor dead from reality.

Orthodox Britain

Audrius Razma

Legal Notice

It's an art of fiction never intended to be a resemblance of living but create an alternative reality parallel to our lives, helping us experience a sensation and entertainment of non-existing events.

If the coincidental information about fictitious forms of work comes into mind, they never intended it to mention neither living nor dead from reality.

Acknowledgements

In the memory of Prince Philip we will take a last ride. The most sincere condolences, let him rest in peace and shine in our memories.

We would also like to appreciate master filmmakers Takeshi Kitano and Guy Richie.

We must remember our godfather of horror movies Rob Zombie, who made a new trend forbidding major actors to survive his thrilling silver screen.

Let's see these twists of fortune capture our imagination.

Author expresses sincere thank you for the Cartels Writers group allowing him to grow and learn to be a writer.

Let's compliment Prowritingaid writing partners in crime.

Manifesto

Three weeks from now prison gates bangs and our Ignacius and Simon are walking into the prison van.

They have just been found guilty of double homicide and they look in awful spirits from the decision in the crown courthouse.

Simon, "Well it was well knowing you Ignacius" he has a black eye and large patch on his chest starting in a middle black going to blue and ending in a yellow circle from the prison beating he had when guards were taking him to court.

Ignacius smiles with a swollen jaw, "I wonder how long it will take before the dentist."

Simon sits in a prison van seat while they park it in the courthouse garage and leans back, "Where the hell is our Mage", he thinks to himself.

Then the prison escort receives the green light to leave the gates and starts its engine. The two prison van guards are heading off, the guard on the passenger seat takes out a bottle of still water from the glove compartment and takes the lid off, he pours the water in his mouth and swallows it, "We have another duty on route, anyway mate it is a pleasure to meet you. I can see you are our new guy here".

The driver takes a turn to Pimlico Street and while he is watching the rear mirror, he can see the guy sitting in blue and white uniform is closing his eyes to slide asleep near the door window, "a pleasure to meet you, I am Mage".

While, across the river where Prison van is heading is Gothminster House of Island Nation. The highest Lord of the House is relaxing in front of his window overlooking the green river. He is thinking to complete and sign executive law paper he is an architect behind the order. The Lord is sitting in red ox blood colour seat made from wooden frame. He places his left arm on carved Demon head before he seals the executive order. He takes off paperwork from red leather table top and leaves it in a red suitcase to hear a knock on his office door, "Your Excellency we are ready to have lunch time", he takes his gaze away from sunshine and takes a sharp look at his attendant, "I am ok to have lunch in office because I need to sign more orders", young attendant replies, "Yes your Excellency David".

A while later the lunch servant walks in to show today's food options and while he is showing the lunch menu to the Excellency, he places his old tired hand in his pocket to pull out his shoelace. He grabs his Excellence on his neck and pulls tight. The executive chair swings from side to side making silent squeaks but he is holding with his knee to make Lord of Gothminster lose his ground on his chair while he is grasping for his air, "I think one rat is done".

***

Ignacius inspects around him and asks Simon where are they taking us while the prison van is heading now in a forest, Simon "I think we are now fugitives running from court cases".

Ignacius, "I would love to have my kebab now."

Simon smiles and licks his lips, "Do you know a good joke about lawyers?".

Ignacius, "I had enough of this law today, you just keep it down."

Simon, "The government lawyers are the law brokers who sell the law and lawyers are those who protect the law."

Ignacius, "I would not mind meeting these brokers to break their bones."

Simon, "I am sure your time comes same as everyone's,"

Ignacius, "good", he shows a thumb up.

***

When Ignacius was thinking about having his fast food on the other side of Crimson Island, the Dark Lord is giving a good beating in his basement to his tied up in chair Foreign Excellency Blond. While Vice Excellency is watching she is feeling tempted by his majesty's supreme powers in a corner and she then craves to offer herself to him, she passes him a towel to wipe blood off his hands. Then she places one hand on FE Blond shoulder and pulls up her office skirt to show the Dark Lord she is not wearing underneath, "o our supreme Lord commander I want you as much as did our Blond, I am sure Mr Blond won't mind it".

He pulls his pants off after he throws a bloody towel on the side of the floor, "I understand you do not love to fail".

Dark Lord takes her waist closer, stretching her to ramp in her backside while she is still holding her hand on her Foreign Excellency shoulders.

***

The twin sisters from Japan have arrived at Crimson Nation Island. Their names were Nami and Yami Suki. They handed their passports and smiled, "Arigato!!", then they took a cab from Central Airport to their Five-Star Hotel suite. The hotel was not far from the Crimson Island Capital tourist spots to enjoy walking street districts.

They were here for romantic dating holidays to find holiday romance while they conduct their original business trip plans.

When Nami is in a shower, Yami is looking out their twin bedroom window into the street lights replacing their daylight, she could see her reflection in the window, making her know she is just as good as her sister.

They had agreed only to one difference: to have ponytail hair and Nami to style piggy tail on her hair.

She can hear the bathroom door open and her sister walks in, only holding her towel. Nami walks closer to her and whispers in her ear, "I still left the shower room all hot and steamy for you, here take my towel or you just would like me to be with me if you wish so, hehehe."

Yami shrugs her shoulders and shakes her head side to side, holding her lips tucked together, "I want my shower too".

Nami smiles, takes a seat on her bed and throws her wet towel on Yami's shoulder, "You better have fun", she crosses her naked legs together. Yami grabs the towel off her shoulder and walks away, feeling in a rush. She walks in the shower room and before she takes a good wash, she takes off her white t-shirt and folds it in a square.

Yami reaches for her black linen trousers buttons and has them off to fold it square next to her t-shirt. With a touch of a finger D Cup bra drops from front of her chest to let her breast slide while she is still holding on her white satin bra, "gosh it was long day and I feel like soaking in today", she says to herself and she folds it in half to place it on her t-shirt.

Yami slaps her butt check while looking at herself in a mirror and takes off her underwear.

The shower curtain pulls wide open, and she walks in the shower, "I hope my lovely sister has not done you dead mister pervert?", in the shower is a lying man. He is bleeding and held together on a single rope.

He is gasping for air through Nami's tucked-in underwear in his mouth and his arms with legs up backwards together making him arch. The rope continues around his neck and over shower curtain rail.

Yami smile and sits on his butt naked making her so small compared to Caucasian man in his 60s with grey hair on his head. Her soft hand brushes over his cheeks for him to close his eyes, "do not worry I have my turn to have my dinner first, she left me for you", she can see him bleeding from short stab wounds around his abdominal sides in three to four places with non-vital stabs.

The curtains close and she adjusts tap water to favourite temperature before she turns on the shower, "about time for my blood bath", steps on with strength on his wounds to see him in eyes and when their gaze meets she smiles, "do not worry lovely", to see him in tears dropping on his cheeks.

Yami pulls the rope while he is attempting to resist and makes muffled sounds. Her body half his height and weight has strength to pull him up above floor level and she ties the rope to the sidebar, leaving him above the floor.

Yami licks his ear and whispers in his ear, "do not worry mister simpleton", brushes her fingers on his neck, "I only willing to love you, remember?", slides below him and pushes his head to gaze between her legs when she picks up razor and cuts his throat open for his blood to drip over her legs.

Yami continues after every kiss to cut around his body, making her become excited and more messaging her fingers into his body. Her face miles, "I want it all", and she slices off one of his testicles to lick her finger with it.

His face in torment makes her continue to smile and she slides her legs open in front of him, while their gaze is together and he has now no more tears in his eyes, she is pulling a nail hammer her sister left her tonight to help have a good bath. Winking her fingers, "bye bye", she starts without stopping, smashing the hammer into his head over his face, when she believed she delivered the final blow she did not stop because knew it was his nerves twitching while she was having her joy.

Her relief to finish him with a good workout made her feel like getting up for a stretch.

She kicked him aside making a way to a rope with his useless head to allow her to reach the knot, "how man can be useless", her pulling rope was making him go further to the ceiling.

The shower was having more hot steam than before when she heard her signal of classical symphony number 5. It was her sister's signal to start her blood bath.

Yami took a grey -colored wooden handle sushi knife, made of fine black Japanese steel you can buy in majority shops in the capital here.

The step back in a hot shower made her soft butt cheek sit; her hands cut his guts open to let his blood and organs mixing with the heat and water fall on her head, reminding her of early spring rain.

The joy of rubbing his insides with blood over her body was worth his life.

Later on, Yami throws her sister's towel back at her, "it was worthwhile the trip." Nami looks at her and smiles, "have you flushed the dirt?", Yami takes a seat on grey sofa and opens a bottle of water, "yes, I cut him to 356 pieces and washed it the drain, but you know how I say if you smile after the dinner.", Nami is laughing, "They will take your teeth out? Oh, and I thought we attended the same assassination school.", Yami makes no comments and closes her eyes for the moment.

***

Into the dark night a campfire is making sparking sounds of fire wood burning and three friends are sitting together on a large piece of driftwood.

Simon takes one piece of sausage and stabs it on a tree branch before placing it on fire, "Did you know that Japanese Shamanism loves to soak the bloodbath of their victims they take to mark Amaterasu?

Ignacius turns to Simon, "Do not tell me shat stories by the fire in the middle of a dark forest at night. I already have bad dreams.", he stabs one sausage too and points it in fire.

Mage smiles, "buuuuuUUUuuu", then looks in a bag for sausage too.

Ignacius, "Ignacius by the way, who the hell is Ameterasu?", he turns his sausage on the campfire to fry it even.

Simon, "She is a goddess of fire."

Ignacius, "Yeah, right. It is like our pagan god of Thunder with his symbol of Oak the tree even thunder cannot break."

Soft sounds of wind brushing against the leaves of forest trees and dead silence besides a couple of Ovals making sounds, the abandoned campsite is a good place to soak in the forest. Prison van is just making a slight noise with the prison guard making sounds of struggle to set himself free from ropes Ignacius has tied to him.

The rest fugitives are in a wooden cabin since their first day out of prison and their first night in a decent bed. They are not even concerned about having their dinner fast asleep.

Crimson Island

Early in the morning Ignacius wakes up other two fugitives to ask them if they agree to train for an important mission for their freedom.

Their names were Bob Jumbo and Dylan Mambo and were eager to start their firearms training with Simon.

The same day Bob told Simon he knows well about masochist FE Blond fashion for fetishism and about eminent torture chambers he likes to get his way.

Later in the day, the training starts and Lord Ignacius takes a cup of fresh water, "Now I miss well our Reno Marihuana from Crimson Prison"

Simon, "I hear they made it well."

They start basic tactical combat training while moving across forest with the raised hand of Simon to the direction every second points their stick to a different side; with another hand gesture they take an aim on one knee.

Mage is observing them from above on the tree branch, having his sandwich and small bottle of water for his lunchtime.

They take lunch break too and Mage points them out on their timing and space control mistakes while they do point of contact training.

Bob Jumbo, "We are like Robin Hood and the boys now taking back from the Sheriff."

Ignacius, "We are little far from them since we do not have any money."

Simon, "how our dear Detective Simpleton is getting on without us."

Ignacius, "he is like a psycho. Do you remember him talking about four archangels, justice, and the rest of weird stuff."

Simon, "how he is planning and why our Vice-Commander draw urgent request to assist him with this mission."

Ignacius, "Yeh we are on a mission impossible déjà vuuuu."

Simon, "I see Crimson werewolf awuuu."

Ignacius, "While coopers of Gothminster arresting a werewolf of capital awwuuuu out of their vans," they all laugh at a good joke.

***

Then later on the day Detective Simpleton was sitting at home and staring in his old painting made from white and black paint.

He never could understand why inherited this painting but he admires day break shadows covering their oil point adding more texture in his living room when Archangel dissents from the sky.

The Archangel closes its black wings and kneels before him, "We have another message for you about apocalyptical justice", Mr Simpleton places his cup of tea and swallows the remaining drop of tea in his mouth.

Simpleton makes a religious gesture and speaks to one of Archangels, "I was fine four weeks ago running my independent agency but four of you guys had to wake me up in a middle of the night about pending disaster and now I have to run errands for you guys like a madman around here."

Archangel with a deep voice announces the message for our Detective Simpleton, "You should know the skies above are pleased you assist us and would like to let you know you must head two o'clock outside Gothminster House of Lords to serve the justice to be continued."

Simpleton takes his check coat and pair of his glasses, "You guys cannot be told difference by looks nor by sound of voice, and always points me in a direction with another mosaic before I leave."

Archangel claps its large wings and before it leaves he says, "Much appreciated from skies above".

Our Detective heads off when he purchases a ticket on a tram and joins aboard to the direction of the Houses of Gothminster stop; while a missing prison transport is heading to the same direction.

The prison transport turns into a straight lane leading straight to House of Gothminster, speeding over speed limit over passing other vehicles like a standstill when they crash through personnel gates in order to the gardens of Crimson Ministry.

They jump out of a blue and white van saying 'Crimson Correctional Transport', and pull out extended cartridge assault rifles, opening live ammunition fire how they did training in the woods. When Dylan cannot open the closed lock, Simon says, "You beat it", when he knocks the door handle down with a firearm handle and kicks the doors open.

The team moves in a straight line holding their firearms over each other's shoulders opening rounds of fire at any member of personnel they can see in their vision.

When the team approaches the stairs, the guards of the House are rushing to the lower floor. Ignacius orders to surround the staircase for tactical ambush and Simons shouts when the House Guards approach their vision, "Attack in Attack!", then they open fire looking through gun triggers aiming every dropped round for contact with headshot.

They move upstairs taking careful steps, bending their knees and pushing with their feet the bodies of dead security personnel, with Mage behind them navigating the tourist map.

Simon, "I am happy today was closed to tourists for renovation needs", Mage continues to browse through the map for the fastest route to the Head of Ministry chambers.

They reach the chambers after quick rounds of fire when they kick the doors open to see the office abandoned in a rush, then Mage radios through a signal, "Bob if you with us you should be able to see outside Prison van a black escort leaving in about five, you can open live round on second transport".

The hand radio is cracking and he can hear Bob's voice, "I thought you guys already forgot about me, I was not even sure these building site walkies-talkies will work.", he pauses for a minute then he continues, "I can see them". The tactical team now in upstairs chambers can hear the sudden gun fire down below when Mage shows a hand signal to leave from Gothminster House.

Yet Simon smashes the office window and opens fire on a second vehicle with a Car15 assault rifle at the vehicle on an escape route, "I am sure our Bob cannot count and I added some ammunition to help our boy". When Simon stops, they make a run down the stairs back through staff rooms towards the van; along the way, Ignacius is counting the dead bodies they left behind in today's countermeasure mission.

They run past a van for Bob to join them together and when they reach the river near House of Gothminster; they take a Police speed boat for their escape transport.

***

The moments before attack FE Blond VE May was having a cup of tea in their chambers boardroom, "It is a sad moment to learn our E David had passed away, we are not sure how to let the nation know about our loss yet", when VE May blinks her eyes and takes her look away from FE Blond, "who is in charge now when your dirty ass gets whipped all the time around when we come to this".

A Terrorist attack interrupted their alarm and left for Gothminster Library's secret passage in the underground car park to board secure vehicles taking them to the Safe House briefing.

VE May fastens her seat belt, "I hate these fools causing havoc around our home", when sudden shots fire from above hits her twice in abdominal and one direct hit in her skull leaving out her jaw, FE Blond takes cover one her lap after he get shot in his shoulder and secure escort non stop drives off to Safe House.

While FE blond is laying on dead body lap and is attempting to regain his mind, he is thinking to himself why he had to agree to put in place his E David unapproved drug trial allowing women medicine causing birth defects; it was his last thoughts before he woke up in Military Security Hospital.

***

When Detective Simpleton made it in time to reach the House of Gothminster, he could see his teammates and other two men making their great escape. He understood they would need his help, and he came home to take his weekend car.

They made it in the 1980s and is wide built, allowing many passengers in sedan versions but due to fuel consumption he did not use it.

He drives along the river to spot similar looking individuals and park right before them along the street, "I am afraid it is only deluxe vehicle service today operating", for them to smile and to board vintage cars.

They make a round turn and drive until they reach the red light. But while still at traffic lights, two police officers approached them on a foot patrol.

The female officer knocks on a passenger window and Dylan lowers the car window door down holding a handgun under his jacket pointing at her through the passenger door.

She smiles and lowers her head to the passenger door, bending her back to her male colleague, "I love your car and could see you took a U-turn in single lane traffic".

Simpleton smiles and makes an apology about a minor traffic violation promising to avoid his mistake, "I am so sorry I was in a hurry to drop off my nephews to football practice, and now I can hear this commotion around.

I was in a hurry to avoid traffic", female officer smiles, "Because I love your car and we are little in a hurry I let you go without a ticket", she turns her eyes up like she would think twice, "But I would love to have your number my dear", and she blinks before she turns around and walks away.

Gothminster

Let's continue following our young guns travelling in the belly of the beast while leaving police lines to not cross in every hot corner.

Meanwhile, in the train station a foreign woman is assaulted on the platform when men are screaming at her while they are attacking her, "Go back home where you come from, you biatch", they are kicking her on the floor while she is helpless gasping for air asking for help.

A week later the region council office worker is passing by with his proud pin badge written on it he is To Be Proud Dark Lord Servant but he does not know he is followed behind by a group of young men, they targeted him down the street when they observed his blue suit.

One of the young men approaches him and asks him if he has a lighter, the Council Officer worker responds he does not smoke and he rather prefers him to walk away.

But the remaining group of young men runs up behind him and places a dirty bin bag over his face. They just took the bag off the nearby bin.

The first young man he approached punches him in a solar plexus, making him lose air and grip on his feet. Then he kicks the officer worker in his head while he is losing his consciousness on his knees and the remaining group kicks him on the floor.

The young man takes a lighter out of his pocket and places his backpack on the floor next to him, "a shame they taught you rubbish in law school."

He opens his backpack and takes out 3 liters cider bottle full of petrol; he pours the petrol over Council Officer workers' body and lights him on fire for him to wake up in agony of fire all over his body; he tries to stand up taking off the bin bag off his face and run but he trips over the platform and is killed by expressway train, making his body torn to many parts.

The young man places his lighter in his pocket and taps his friends over their shoulders, "very great work lads when we serve our community just right", they all walk away laughing.

***

The same day when the incident took place in the capital's outskirts train station, not far away in Crimson Island, the army hospital is recovering FE Blond. He opens his eyes and can see a nurse near him; he taps his palm on her bottom while she is taking a reading from the life support monitor and orders her to bring in a doctor in charge of his care.

While he smiles he says to himself, "I am lucky now the entire country is in my hands."

When she comes back with his doctor, FE Blond learns he was lucky to escape a fatal wound because the firearm bullet went through his arm clean but the doctor announced his female colleague was fatally wounded.

FE Blond sits with the help of his nurse and tastes his cup of tea, "I am sad about such horrors we experienced as a country, I must request an immediate visit from police and army chiefs to see me, due to the sad deaths of my superiors I am now the leader of Crimson Nation."

While the military hospital was arranging an emergency summit not far away, three friends were camping and cooling down their feet in cold water.

Simon, "I wonder how long we need to stay low in our campsite before the next expedition to resume the order our Simpleton has drafted us for?"

Mage, "I am not sure because I cannot contact our HQ since we made an entry."

Ignacius, "so strange we have gone through so much but not much avail to stop the evil deeds."

Simpleton walks up to them on lake pier and asks them to follow him to the cabin where Dylan and Bob are waiting to further plan how to restore order for them to complete their mission.

While on the other side of the capital Yami and Nami are walking to their prearranged date with the lovely police officer, they find him on a local dating application on their mobile.

Yami, "I wonder what kind of candy is our mister police officer."

Nami, "I am sure he is sweet as a candy in our mouth", then she licks her lips and both girls laugh.

They come near the station of the wild nature park and are waiting outside the bus stop where the police officer promised blind double date.

The black limousine stops near them and the passenger seat window pulls down for them to learn their double date inside their car.

The men were joking when driving to the natural reserve site about their date and how they will get quick sex in back of their car and they later toss these stupid girls far away, making them walk back all the way they came.

Then when the car window pulls down Nami waves a brown hair man, and Yami blinks her left eye before they board the government issued transport.

They drive a single kilometer further to the car park before they park in an unused road under construction, Nami switches seats with the driver to sit closer with the police chief and his driver takes the back seat closer to Yami.

Nami smiles and brushes his suit and tie rubbing his left leg closer to his groin but she pulls tight a knot of his tie twisting his gaze to the passenger seat for spills of blood drop on his face.

The blood is coming from his driver's mouth while all arteries on his neck and blood vessels on his face are turning black and Yami is holding his driver by his throat.

Yami pulls a tie towards her and turns the Police Chief gaze to her, "That snot nose thought he would blaze in our stomach. But how about you?"

She pulls out her lollipop, pops out her mouth with her left arm from his hip and stabs him two times in his groin.

She pulls his tie over her shoulder, meeting their shoulder together in a hug, she places her mouth closer to his ear, "Shhh do not worry".

Then she rubs her arm from his groin to his stomach up and down, for the poison to flow quicker. He dies in her arms.

When Yami and Nami finish pulling dead bodies in the trunk of their car, Yami checks their wallets, "Great, we just finished the Police Chief and his driver."

Nami smiles and kicks their legs in to close the trunk, "we inherited their wheels on our first date".

She shouts out of happiness and jumps up clapping her hands in the air, "we will now not need to walk around now".

Yami, "Great, I am already tired."

The poison was from black crab, the nerves paralysis poison only found in their native home shores.

They dip the needles in a pure extract of black crab venom and concealed them inside sticks of sweets they packed inside their bag before their flight.

The poison is the strongest in the entire world, making a man's heart stop in three seconds from nerve paralysis, and since so effective no one ever had an idea to create an antidote for the venom.

While the girls boarded their borrowed government vehicle and were placing their make-up looking at the rear mirrors of their vehicle, on the other side of the triangle of location point; Simon was opening a tin of black shoe wax.

He dips his two fingers inside the tin and is making straight line marks on his face, then brushes wax off with a wet towel and places another direction of shoe wax once more.

Mage walks in to see Simon using shoe wax, "ok to adjust war paint to your face contours but do not forget we will end up without if you use it all."

Simon turns around, "Do not worry, I am almost done."

Mage looks at him from the chair. He places his feet on the table and inspects Simon's face, "Well done, you look great."

Simon Says, "Let's show them northern European mind games."

Mage, "Well better than Ignacius painting black only his eyes and his lips."

**

Two weeks after the disappearance of the Police Chief with his driver and FE Blond resuming powers of his nation, now he is Excellency Blond and is making an appearance with his financial donors in a government owned golf course.

Sinbury

When Simon approaches His Excellency golf course, he shows them the Art of War and takes the Excellency in for questioning about his intentions to the Nation.

Ignacius is walking next to Simon. He has cast clay arm over his left arm with bandage over it to keep it straight over his shoulder.

Ignacius, "The bottles you", before Simon looks around how to infiltrate pass security and exit routes to have Blond handed back in their camp.

Simon walks past the alleyway and picks up an empty bottle of wine. He relaxes his shoulders and sways his arms to sides when he walks up to security guards.

He walks up a meter apart from the guard at the side entrance and sways over the head of security guards to see how the second security officer reaches for his hand radio with the intention to press the panic button.

Ignacius spends no time waiting and hits the guard over his face with a cast clay arm, he rushes in his right arm in a cast clay arm and slashes over the neck of the security officer. Ignacius is standing there and is catching his breath with a long slim blade in his hand. The blood splatters from the cut are just leaking off the wooden doors.

The entrance is not a common type to enter the golf field; it is at the end of a small alleyway, made of a stone wall covered in moss and reaffirmed by a steel, wooden door.

Simon takes out two rain jackets from his backpack and handles one to Ignacius.

Ignacius, "I now cursed us dagger daggering Crimsoners?"

Simon inspects Ignacius' right hand, "I think you would fit the description far better than me".

Simon places his bottle in a backpack and takes out a tin of black shoe wax.

He places two lines across his face of shoe wax.

Then he passes the shoe wax to Ignacius to see him draw black circles around his eyes and on his lips.

Simon, "We will need to keep our heads low under our coats until we reach Blond, then war paint across our faces will distort our images in their security cameras, giving better chances not to be detected."

Ignacius, "I am sure my face paint will give them creeps."

Simon, "I felt uncomfortable already."

They jump over a stone fence since they could not find the keys and continue walking along the bushes and ponds looking around for a blonde man.

His Excellency Blond at the time went inside the top floor of the golf course building to toast a glass of champagne with his financial donors. He was talking about the next election strategy and his great past success, making him leader of Crimson Nation.

His speech did not go ahead so well as he planned because Simon and Ignacius were looking through glass doors in the balcony to make sure it was him who would be taken together with them to their campsite.

Simon throws in a steel chair from the balcony to allow them access to the lounge and create a diversion of confusion, the element of surprise they needed to successfully capture His Excellency.

When E Blond hears the sounds of shattering windows, he screams to sound the alarms and his bodyguards rush him and VIP guests to the rooftop of the building. It was all according to Blond's plan.

When he learned they nearly shot him dead from above him when he was escaping Gothminster, he ordered his security to give him other security plans rather than the last failed ones.

Simon is wasting no time and enters the scene of chaos. The staff and guests are covering their heads in a rush from sides to sides.

The moment of despair allows Simon to manipulate bodies, pushing them in the way of guards when he hits them over their heads with his wine bottle, then he reverses and smacks his elbow in the security's face.

He takes his deep breath and kicks the table over to shield his stance.

He does a 360 degree round house kick in the guard's head walking behind the table. He trips over another guard with the same table he kicked over.

Simon picks up the table by its legs because he can see most of the guests have evacuated and now is wide enough open space for them to use their firearms.

He rushes the table to the remaining security, pressing them to open the doorway.

The image is indescribable, such as a painting of war; the bodies of ten men one over another attempting to weigh down Simon just to give them their space to reach their holster.

Ignacius is wasting no time and starts running across a long table with his feet kicking aside all the drinks and meals left on the plates.

He attempts to jump over Simon, only landing a hard elbow and breaking the jaw of security. But he did not come empty-handed and stabbed him in the neck with his concealed blade.

Ignacius does not stop with a single strike of his blade and continues stabbing them across their jaws, necks, ears and eyes for Simon to realise the pressure pushing his end of the table is decreasing.

Ignacius pushes Simon aside from the table, "Let me cleanse this well."

He then continues stabbing into the table until he understands there is no more gasping, there is no more struggle on the other end of their table.

Simon quickly leans hard against the wood table side and makes a run to the top floor, looking for His Excellency.

Excellency Blond is taking a shelter under large clay flower basins with his two top donors, their names are Mr Bill and Mr Merlin. He is leaning behind the basin and is looking at how security personnel are pointing their handguns towards the doors.

He taps back on Mr Bill and nods looking at them, "Do not worry, everything will be great. I am not for no reason the number one leader of our nation."

When he can hear loud breathing behind his back and smoothing dripping on the tile floor. When he looks back, it is too late because Ignacius was standing right behind him.

His Excellency screams only to learn Ignacius pulls him back, taking him for a live shield and having a sharp blade covered in blood pointing across his neck.

When security understands the gravity, they are standing and turning their handguns around.

Simon kicks the door open pushing one guard over the floor and before the second guard makes his way back pointing his gun to Simon, he hits him over his head with a bottle of wine.

While he dazed the guard from the blow to his skull, Simon takes his right arm pointing towards the floor and squeezes his finger to fire a shot to the chest.

The direct shot penetrates one security officer's chest, but Simon takes no chances and presses his foot on the firearm that is left on the floor.

He three seconds later kicks aside the gun he was holding under his foot, and twists the hand of the officer's hand he is holding.

They walk and from the twist from his neck to his right arm finger tips pain is unbearable causing him to drop his gun.

Simon continues walking towards kicking his knees down the legs of the security guard, walking past Ignacius and throws the guard off the balcony.

Mr Bill and Mr Merlin looked below them from the balcony to see what they left of security to keep them safe.

When he was falling down he hit his skull hard enough on the side of the building to reveal the insides of his head, then he fell on an enormous gap between the pool floor and steps to tables.

His legs were turned left and his neck was so stretched on the sidewalk it was obvious enough it got detached from the spine.

When Ignacius orders Blond to move and keep his mouth shut, Mr Bill grabs a brick from the side of a large clay basin and aims for his head.

But Simon kicks him aside, making a path for Ignacius to continue escorting their hostage.

He takes no further chances and grabs Bill on the side of his neck and pushes him through a glass rail to meet the same fate they had just witnessed.

Simon took a quick look below him to understand the same brick had in his hand now was in Merlin's hand aiming back of his head.

He ducked the blow to the back of his skull and kicked Merlin's feet, making him lose his balance. While Merlin was taking a second to regain his balance, Simon pulled his arm towards the glass railing and pushed his neck in shards of broken glass.

Simon kicked Merlin's neck deeper in broken glass, leaving his dying eyes looking down below him.

Ignacius was standing to doorway to stairs and was punching Blond in his stomach, "Simon, hurry, I know shat happens but if we do not hurry, we will cover more casualties along the way!"

Simon spat down below and rushed towards Ignacius to help him secure His Excellency and head back to their campsite to start his interrogation.

Simon throws F Blond in the back of his car trunk, "You cannot do this to me, I study law university and I am a leader of this supreme nation", Simon shuts the trunk.

Ignacius, "Yeah right, he is lucky for now not to end up like Bill Twatter and Merlin D Cup", he smiles when they walk to board Blond's escort vehicle.

Simon, "I study life's university."

Ignacius before takes a passenger seat, slaps the trunk a couple times and says, "Good luck, my friend."

The Sinbury, Boys!

The night before our heroes are interrogating His Excellency Blond Da Dirta Cossack, somewhere on the motorway is speeding a thunder truck with a sticker written on it: Power-Up.

Simon the night before was dreaming about a giant cat burning the world with a strike of match and he is afraid every night the nightmares will continue.

But now they throw Blond on the floor in a campsite cabin for Bob and Dylan to kick him on the floor, the kicks are turning so violent Blond is thinking his guts will burst open his sides are stinging so much. But Bob and Dylan are not thinking to stop warming him until they acknowledge a puddle of blood coming out from their enemy.

Mage walks in and places his mug of coffee before he tells them to stop beating him and take him to the lake pier for fresh midnight water. "I prefer him to have a good wash to see his face telling the truth before us rather than him dead in a pile of his own shat in our cabin."

They pull Blond on his legs outside the cabin towards the lake, spitting on him along the way because he is moaning about the injuries he sustained at the start of their inquiry to his plans.

He opens his swollen eyes up when they take a bin bag off his head and he can see the stars from above the night sky. He can feel his arms and legs tied up to a metal chair.

His body temperature is far greater at the moment than the rusty metal chair they trapped him in, and he does not feel at ease.

Mage slaps him across his face two times, feeling the blood on his hand from his bleeding face.

"I hope you rather stop stargazing tonight or I murder you on the spot before you spill the beans of your evil deeds."

"I swear it was the Dark Lord and his Evil Viking Princess.

They contemplated selling unapproved medicines to pregnant women causing birth defects and the former Excellency of Crimson

Nation, our David, covered the case up by sending the victims to a madhouse."

"I assume you were an underdog assuming nothing about it and only pushing the pencils to make your career goals go further?"

"I swear it was not me, I only did what I was told."

But Simon smiles and walks one step closer. He steps over a metal chair and smacks his boot in Blond's neck.

"I am sure you are no good fool, same as your forefathers, to be proud satanic island nation supreme commanders who started two global wars and massacred many nations of people leaving piles of corpses behind them."

Then he watches how E Blond is gasping for air from his wide open throat. He turns around holding his heel on his crushed throat and feels how his stomach is growling inside him.

"Because your ancestors displaced the entire planet's population in poverty and death so you could be proud at least I can feel your mouth with my warm shat, matey." He lets his belt slip and drops his butt cheeks on Blond.

He felt a relief only for a moment Simon's foot came off his dry throat but now he can't breathe much longer feeling feces floating down his mouth, overflowing from sides of his mouth causing him gasping chokes on his throat.

Simon stands up and watches how the wild eyes of His Excellency Blond have lost its focus. His throat is throwing hick-ups, flowing feces and his stomach content out of his mouth for another try to live one. "I am sorry mates, I could not hold myself together allowing him to set free, I wanted to know he had good feed at yesterday's banquet."

Magnum Mage walks over his stomach heading back to the cabins and while he is walking away, he asks his mates to dip into the water with their Excellency Blond for a good wash before they load him up back into their truck.

They tie the knot of the rope to their chain and Ignacius kicks a metal chair over into the lake to pull back up afloat and merge him under the water. "This shat bag is hell heavy."

***

Our Bob Mumbo and Dylan Jumbo were Crimson Nation Sumo Federation leaders, and had the nickname Demolition Brothers for their own reason.

Mage was driving their black truck and was learning further about their destined new teammates. He was picked up from Crimson Prison.

They learned through Detective Simpleton the mental health hospital in Sinbury is keeping victims of illegal drugs from Dark Lord imprisoned under false claims they were insane.

They pull to third gear and drove Capital Road A30 leading to Sinbury to meet their future perspectives Detective Simpleton recommended for his biblical justice prevail.

***

Simon was already in Sinbury before the rest of the heroes arrived at the location Simpleton told to operate a commando mission and walked into a local firearms store.

"I wonder how many crowns it would be for this pellet rifle on display." He points his finger at camouflage model 300X, with a high velocity sniper frame gun with a sticker on it stating it was great for scaring crows of your trees.

The gun store keeper passes a pellet rifle to Simon and lets him know today they are having 10% sale if he purchases it with a 2000 pallet package.

"What a focking sale mate!" He smacks the store keeper in the face with the other end of his rifle and jumps over the counter, hitting him over the head.

"It is a focking sale matey." He continues beating the gun seller, hitting his skull with his thick boots.

He then walks up to the store front and flips the sign over to the store that is closed and closes the lock behind him.

"As we say where I am from, I was not born on a bus." He walks up to the unconscious but still breathing gun store keeper and takes him back to the storage room to find these 2000 pallets he promised him 10% discount.

Simon walks out back of the store and looks up to the sunny skies above Sinbury, aims and fires at the town square circle made out steps made to sit and have lunch for local office workers.

He licks his finger to see the wind direction and counts his breath by the wind speed, observing local wind breeze coming through two to three-storey buildings round the main town square.

"Business as usual."

When he is 30 meters away from town square, a car park is on the second floor above the supermarket.

He takes a short walk thinking the perfect wind direction will help him fire and aim at the Crimsoners at town Square.

He takes two streets left, believing he will make it in time to reach his spot to open fire, but he notices a man standing at a cash machine near the car park.

The man is looking right at him, observing Simon. He sights, "I think I start sooner rather than later." Simon waves at a man crossing his path, "Hey old man!"

He throws his rifle forward, "Catch it mate." Simon rushes up to him while the rifle lands in man's hands. He kicks his boot tip in his groin and snatches his rifle back from his hands.

Simon hits him over his face with his rifle. He takes a step aside and hits his happy customer two times in the neck, smashing his head further in a cash machine cracking its screen.

"I am sure that one will be attempted robbery.", when he walks away from his first happy customer.

He walks up the stairs and then he aims and fires with every breath he takes.

Shooting one office worker's ear off, he hits one in his hand and fires a third shot in his ass while there is panic in the town square between officer workers scattering them and running with panic.

Simon takes a seat and opens a can of soda water to see how fast they will find in the car park but before he finishes his drink the firearms officers locate and surround him, "Hands on your head and drop to the floor!"

He takes advice from firearms officers and kneels down the floor holding his hands above him.

When he walks up before the judge, crown prosecution announces charges and brief history of his case, "This man is a wanted fugitive, our dear justice, he committed homicide and assisted in another homicide with another fugitive in the wanted criminals list."

Simon's lawyer takes defence and asks him to be detained before we will hold further medical advice upon crown courthouse.

He then asks Simon to take a stand in the witness box to speak his statement in order for the judge to process his case.

Simon walks the aisle with heavy steel cuffs on his both hands and feet, he steps in a witness box and scratches his forehead, "I only wished to make my customers happy, I was working so long keeping shoes clean my dear liege, and I aimed hard to keep it this way."

The judge looks to the defence lawyer and asks him to explain the speech the defendant had just said, "I hope I satisfied you or would like to hear the defendant's further thoughts on his statement."

But before the judge places his hammer, "I am from Ruso planet and I love outstanding women like your daughter, mister judge."

Then the judge shouts it is enough of this and orders him to keep two weeks in high restriction local asylum to see how he will respond to treatment before he can make further decisions.

Sinbury at Midnight

They summoned Simon up to the crown's courthouse, and Ignacius was holding plans for the battle of his own.

He was sitting and thinking how Mage is doing with Bob and Dylan to dump His Excellency's body to northern marshes to make him walk back all his way back to Crimson Capital.

The sun was strong, and he was feeling the warmth in his body on the beach near Sinbury. He would rather turn around on his back and have more sunshine before he takes his part in a commando mission.

The Curse Dagger operation in his mind was too much to handle, but he knew it would determine the fate of the satanic island nation.

His wrist watch alarm beeped twice, and he had to be up from comfortable dunes of sand. He hoped on his bike that within 45 minutes of cycling he would reach the destination.

Sinbury was a low profile rural town, but after Simon's attack it was so silent it felt to Ignacius, he could slice such thick silence with his knife.

While picking up speed on the bicycle lane, Ignacius pulls out behind his leather belt a sharp sushi knife he bought in Crimson Capital.

Ahead of him was cycling to medical emergency response cyclists because of the heat wave that day on patrol in case of heat stroke.

"Screw you perverts!" Ignacius shouts and slashes, passing by one of the first responders' neck while the second is attempting to provide first aid. Ignacius stabs him, piercing the tip of his blade through the chest.

"I knew this would make a scene on camera.", speaks under his breath and starts cycling away.

He was right and security cameras captured the incident and filmed a clear picture of Ignacius' face.

It took not long before police officers apprehended Ignacius when he made couple cuts through their vests.

Our Ignacius in the courthouse case has pleased prosecution to provide another suspect of murder.

Their officers captured the fugitive on the run.

"I am an actor and I was filming pornography scenes. I plea not guilty and I shall sleep with your wife if you wish me so, dear court liege!"

But the judge had no excuses and ordered pretrial for mental health tribunal hearing after two weeks investigation in a top security unit.

***

The same night when two patients were administered to a mental health hospital, they found His Excellency Blond naked wandering in the woods and summoned to explain himself to his Dark Lord.

He walks in the chambers of Dark Castle and kneels on his knees before his liege to say, "I regret my failures, your majesty."

The Dark Lord is having a glass of fine wine and on his knees is sitting his blonde mistress. He orders his women to step aside while he inspects in the eyes of this fool.

He stands up and slaps the bottom of his mistress, "My dear Viking Princess, let me set this straight or we will have less time to bathe."

Then walks up to Blond and picks him up on his jaw to smack him hard in his face, but mister Blond thinks to himself it was not as painful as how these fugitives kicked his guts.

"Do you understand why we keep you alive!"

"We need you to cover up after us, like a singer in our toilet singing for us while we feel a need to have a dump on his face!"

"You complete fool, clowns can do better than you to make me angry!"

Dark Lord smacks Blond in his stomach and drops him on the floor.

"I would shag Vikings Princess, you watching us, but I am afraid I would strangle you after, you incompetent fool!"

Meanwhile, the Dark Lord leads his Viking Princess to natural roman baths to have a night filled with pleasure. On the other side of the Nation, Yami and Nami are making a prayer.

Yami and Nami kneel before a large stone, and light their match to set a small fire out of driftwood as they gather inside the Dark Woods Forest.

"You think it will keep their bodies warm."

Nami inspects the distance between two dead bodies they hang upside above their stone altar and fire set above a large stone.

"I am sure it will be enough distance to stop them setting on fire."

"The stars are so bright tonight, it is the perfect shape to complete our ritual for Bakura."

The Bakura, Yami was referring to as their God of Necessary Evil they must offer dead bodies of victims they killed before the gods from above shall approve their wishes come true.

"I think it is enough", Yami says, and lights a torch. She pushes burning wood off the stone and stamps on it with foot to stop fire spreading further and places matcha tea bowl under their dead bodies.

Nami takes a step closer and stabs dead men in their necks, allowing their blood to drip in a large tea bowl underneath them. They both smile, share a round cup of black blood and kiss each other on the lips.

"I think the last part was unnecessary", and they both start laughing after their Pagan God ritual is complete.

***

The time twin sisters finished their ritual, Simon was trying to close his eyes in the government hospital bed. He felt so uncomfortable he could not close his eyes in this ward. The place seemed wrong, and he could not understand it yet.

One of the ward nurses on patrol was completing his rounds of checks before he signed off on his duty. He was taking a step closer to a room Simon was in.

He opened the door hatch and turned the light on to inspect how the new patient was doing.

"Mate, are you ok, I hope you feel comfortable here."

"Hey mate, speak up!"

He takes out his key and opens the door to Simon's bedroom. He walks closer to his bed, not taking his eyes away from the duvet he is covered up in.

His hand is sliding to his pocket, and he is taking out a syringe of venom the Dark Lord Castle's servant gave him before his day on duty, with instructions to stab Simon in his neck.

One meter apart from him and Simon, he jumps on top of his bed and stabs through the duvet in the syringe, letting the venom out.

But Simon was no fool that night and he doubled up his duvet to hide himself aside from the edge of his bed.

Simon kicks the nurse off his bed and stops him breathing, suffocating him with a knee on his windpipe. Simon stands up and takes the keys of the dead body.

"I am sure I could use a tour before my team arrives."

He walks down the corridor at night to open the fire exit door and walks two floors below to the women's ward to see a picture in horror.

Three men are making fun out of their patient. They have her on the pool table, both legs apart.

Two are holding her both arms apart while the other is sticking his insides in-between her legs.

"I can see you are saying you are not insane. Try saying this to your doctor", he says, while he is laughing together with his fellow nurses and pushing deeper and harder inside her.

Simon takes a moment to look and starts walking towards them along the way, taking with him a pool table bat.

He walks up behind the nurse with his pants down and stabs him in butt.

The half-naked nurse is screaming in agony and pushes away from his patient.

But he does not stop and grabs him around his neck with his bat.

"You should lick it clean when ya fock up matey", Simon says, and he pushes the nurse's face between her legs the same moment breaking his neck on the pool table.

Two other nurses let go of the patient's hands and started walking toward Simon. He hits one nurse over his face and breaks his bat and hits the third villain approaching him.

The group of nurses rushes out the emergency exit door and Simon throws his half broken bat across the hall to stab the first nurse in her eye to the doors of the emergency exit.

But to Simon's demise the poor girl who abused picked up a pool ball and hit his head behind him over five times to make him pass away.

The moment he died the clocks stopped and black smoke started coming out behind hall doors. Nurses ignored the surrounding moment while they were attempting to restrain the poor victim of violence.

"You all are fools and rapists", she was screaming her lungs out. But the moment a black figure appeared opposite her in full steel armour, she froze in fear.

The figure thought to himself, in what time and era I wonder in my sleeps on stones of time he traveled.

"Who dares to call his majesty of Grand Duchy", when he says, all the nurses stop restraining the patient and turn back frozen in fear.

He looks at them and with a gesture on the palm of his hand they kneel before him, unable to bear the weight of their bodies on the floor. He continues watching them in silence.

"What a focking freak are now on loose?" One nurse pushes his words out of his throat.

"I can sense the sex magic of these fools", the Grand Duke says to himself and the Pagan Lord necromancer, with the swing of his finger to side, wakes up Simon from dead.

He then points his finger to the nurses and Simon attacks them, massacring them to pieces, ripping with his abnormal human strength apart their organs in his blood thirst.

Simon can see himself from inside him but he cannot gather the moment he feels weak and now sees his body moving on its own, killing with supreme strength those nurses and the patient too many bits.

"Now sleep my son, I blessed you with the sign of Grand Duke's crest", when the ancient Lord Necromancer relaxes his hand Simon falls deep into sleep.

When he wakes up in the morning in a padded cell, he cannot place pieces of puzzle together from a new dream he had.

Sinbury Screams!

The knock wakes up Simon in his blue padded cell. His head is feeling from last night and the dream he had was nothing usual, at least he thought.

The cell hatch opens up and the ward nurse announces the ward doctor is ready to see him for a ward round. The nurse says, "If you are feeling stable and sound for our visit let us know."

Simon turns around under the blanket and nods his head. His eyes are feeling drowsy, he can open the lids of his eyes to see them.

The doctor walks in the blue room after nurses secure the safe space to talk with their patient Simon. Doctor says, "I heard you last night had some trouble sleeping and caused an emergency state in our facility."

"It was black magic."

"I am sure it was. I would like to know more about it.", says the doctor, nodding his head to the nurse taking her notes. But Simon refuses to talk more and closes his eyes. He faces the other side of the room and falls fast asleep.

Meanwhile, our friend Ignacius is just settling down and not wanting to lose time is gathering information from the mental health ward he is located just a floor above Simon is captive.

He asks many questions but cannot establish any truth further from irrational talks he is having with his fellow captives in Sinbury Hospital.

Until he meets Marciuszawa, the student who is for violent behaviour for breaking several laws including anti-social behaviour, body harm and resisting arrest.

He was breaking conditions of bail. The courthouse held him to establish why he was keen enough not to comply and was on a law-breaking spree, increasing his chance to be detained further.

They found common ground after a couple cups of tea and a packet of cigarettes they smoked on the ward balcony. He understood it was taboo for male patients to learn what was in the female ward, causing more causes for concerns.

***

It took a couple days after they parked the thunder truck in a hangar outside Sinbury plains for Mage to establish local support to rescue his fellow teammates from being held captive under courthouse order.

Detective Simpleton pointed him to look for student Daku Stix in the local bar. He felt like in a pub crawl, but when he was about to give up with Bob and Dylan, the luck had made its way.

Daku Stix was philosophy faculty student, spending most of his evenings in union bars before heading out to illegal students' garage fights to earn his title after graduation as King of Hades, in Greek mythology known as underworld for dead.

He and his fellow students were now in the second year of their degree exchanging fists with their fierce rivals from law faculty. But he was having problems because they detained one of his fellows in Sinbury Asylum, and he was eager enough to set him free.

Mage walks in and sits down at the bar. He asks for a double shot of whiskey with no ice. The barman pours a glass and passes to Mage, he twists whiskey glass and pours some in his throat.

"I heard you are in your second year, Stix. I think we have some common ground here to talk business."

"I think you should go where you came from", said Stix.

"I know Marciuszawa's story and who is behind it but I am happy enough to aid you in breaking him out of that shat hole they call Hospital."

Stix orders his fellow students to sit back. He then offers a drink to Mage and asks him to step outside alone to smoke a cigarette with him in case they forge common ground.

***

The nights were getting worse for Simon after he witnessed his own death, and how he came back to life was haunting him the last three nights. He paid little attention to the screams coming from other wards but something occupied enough of him in his mind, what happened to his body he could escape death.

When he can hear along the wind a soft whistling sound coming outside his window. He can recognize the person.

Then Simon took a glimpse at moving shadows along the fence and could recognize Simon with his crew from prison, he was sure they had extra few more bodies moving along them.

When in front of the main entrance two drunk students stumble on the front steps and start urinating on main entrance doors crossing their urine streams together, one saying, "We made an X mark on the devil's gatehouse?"

It took not long before security responded through the doors asking them to leave or they would inform the police about them.

Stix gives a sly smile out of the corner of his lips and says to his fellow student he should not cross his path with this Cerberus.

"Izanagi, have you lost your mind bringing me to the gatehouse of Cerberus?"

He then punches his fellow student to the floor and then punches security guards too back to the walls, kicking and punching them splatters of blood from their broken bones.

Daku waves holding the keys in his hands for his new friends to come out behind the bushes.

He smiles and picks up Izanagi off the floor, dusting him off.

"I am a great actor Daku, your poor punch did me no good or you are just getting weaker after every shot of whiskey."

"I hope I forget what you said next weekend in the union bar, Izanagi."

They open the front gates and step in when Mage, with the rest of the guys, catches up to them at the main doors. Mage says, "Boys, we are making history here."

They inspect blueprints Detective Simpleton emailed them before tonight's fight and they split in a group, making their way in main stairs and fire exit stairs to block any attempt to escape.

Daku and Izanagi are leading their rescue party through main stairs to take back Marciuzawa, when Mage with his team are heading back to free Ignacius and Simon, including witnesses they find for operation the Cursed Dagger to finish.

The screams came out from the asylum but enough patients became quiet listening to their wardens screaming in agony and fear, when assailants were screaming at them giving the beating of their lifetime.

When our heroes are making their way up the floors, nurses fall through the windows dropping on fences or cars breaking their backs.

The dead bodies bleed out their mouths, dilated iris staring up above them, when their fingertips pointing up above them.

It was visible that others did not meet their painless death and were lying on the concrete floor with broken limbs and bleeding to death from brain damage before they found them in a morning shift.

While Ignacius was sharing his last smoke with Marciuzawa, they were observing the wardens heading in panic along the corridors when sirens were beeping without a break.

Then all they can hear windows smashing and Bob with Dylan walking and smiling to them, waving their hands as they were on a usual day visit to see their friends in a hospital ward.

Ignacius' mouth opens so wide and he can see behind them Magnum Magen with Simon Says walking along them and many other men dusting debris off their shoulders.

Marciuszawa screams he was right and philosophers cannot die because they are living proof.

Ignacius looks at Marciuzawa with surprise and comes to understand he was the only one making sense here, who said his friends will storm in here to have him back.

"But why did you tell me it was Hades' Kingdom? I am sure it is sort of graveyard sounding place."

"Junior student, you have much yet to learn."

Then Marciuzawa walks to his mates, giving them a big hug and starts walking away, tapping on each other's shoulders.

Ignacius looks at Mage, Simon, Bob and Dylan to ask them if they have finished the Cursed Dagger project.

"Do we have any intel yet because I am afraid I will catch cancer in my lungs if I stay a day longer in this place?"

Mage says, "We have set all the victims free and told them to wait a couple streets further away from the local park for Detective Simpleton to pick them up and hide them in our new safe house."

But Simon was feeling a withdrawal effect and still holding on his blanket over his shoulders, was thinking about Grand Duke and intention of his appearance the moment he died.

"What is next?"

Sinbury Scares

"The one shall unseal under heavenly gates pass seven passages the seal to set free what they kept seeing us from unseen powers." Our Detective Simpleton wrote a text message to Mage after another vision could be seen from Archangels.

He said to research their former because pure evil of all kinds will deal in supreme matters but Mage could not understand his next mission point he received in his mobile.

"Ok guys, we have further plans and it is time to move out before we have time."

The nuclear Nottingham Power Station disaster the same day struck the news about an accident related to computer system malfunction but before it was the truth.

Time came over Dark Woods forest clouds to cover in heavy matter and Simon sneezed the evening feeling being watched.

Far away in a forest of large smog of dark fumes gathered and a shadow figure appeared in full black armour.

"I can see life and the force of negative energy in my dreams."

He gathered his right hand in a fist, concentrating on a ball of forbidden arts, concentrating the dark fume round his fist in electrifying focus.

It all turned into a large energy ball bewildering, turning against the axis of earth round his hand and when he released it in the palm of his hand, it disappeared into thin air.

The moment it went to sense the force of energy, it was intentional, too.

Meanwhile, at the Nuclear Management Office the nuclear panel safety worker was checking the late night shift and was taking notes of the check screen showing levels of radioactive energy bars in the safe zone when it came he did not expect.

"Mike, I am almost done with the shift controlling the emergency readings department, but when management will send John to cover the next 12 hours I could take time off?"

When his radio started receiving interference and signal sounds made cracking noises in his control management office appeared papers to lift off his table and a thin black ball appeared in mid air above him.

The Daily Crimsoners newspaper published a headline about unprecedented scale calamity stroke Crimson Nation.

Nottingham Power nuclear reactors melted in extreme overdrive and with radioactive conflagration caused massive explosions turning the site to ground zero, not leaving stone on stone making it a large dark hole below the ground it stood once.

The newspaper printed a suggestion Ministry for Crimson Energy Development Department assume preliminary findings of system mellification from computer systems failure to detect overheating overseeing cooling fan system one causing chain reaction in one blast devastating expansion reaching the time clouds above location.

When Simon read the news he said to himself he had enough of those bad feelings and it is time to penetrate further on his mission to eradicate evil, but he asked himself why he had to do it?

It is such a strange task from a detective who seemed not fit into any type of asylum.

He shook his head and continued his focus sitting by the table watching Mage briefing over the map in the middle of the table discussing the next expedition mission.

"Guys I hold a good idea about dealing final blows to these sick leaders."

Lord Ignacius reassured his plans can tackle the crimes of the Nation.

He suggested the following steps reaching above actions in mind of NATO's private security commanding officer's plans.

"I would like to like this Blond's ass on a pick once I finish playing with his wife's boobs."

"You are sicko Ignacius."

"No guys."

"You know what sadistic pervert he is. I gather that he loves to play with his wife his chikdren to see children."

"And?"

"I am sure our lovely officer Simon could pay a visit to his lonely wife at Tvartas way 10 to be of some help."

"No way!"

"You get to wear your uniform back."

"Ok."

There our young officer went to a plan befitting the most unimaginable ways of collecting the truth from sinister.

He knocks on Tvartas Way 10 asking for a cup of tea because he is feeling cold and lonely outside.

"Hello there. Where is your colleague, James? He is regular on duty."

"Mam I think he left on urgent duty and I am only here to complete security checks."

"Oh, come in there I will make a proper tea bag for you."

"I would love you to tea bag it". He then licks his lips and walks in to see her.

While original officers on duty are resting in peace with stab wounds in their heads.

***

Meanwhile Simon is pumping his Excellency Blond's wife on their bedroom table.

Yami and Nami Suki had completed their calling for God's Bakura ritual and to seal their final oath path to complete vowing of necessary evil for an unjust act.

"I am happy about it."

"You sure it will cut it?"

"Yep, it should be enough to send of evil Viking princess back home in her suitcase so they could make a statue back out of her."

"Ok but you make sure it cuts well enough, the last time I had my shoulder sore from an extra hand job."

They both laughed once Yami said it.

The time Simon gave a second shot, moaning, his ending of Kurvaa Jensen's face.

"What a strange name is Kurvaa."

"I think because it sounds nice."

"Ok Kurvaa whatever, now you lick my balls off at once."

"Oh, what a stallion you, mister officer?"

"You just call me Stanley."

He grabs her by her hair and rubs her face in it, thinking to himself she told him about her fool, everything he needs to know.

She was moaning so loud in the heart of public office with her children sleeping below.

He had his fun and left to report his finding to commanding officer Mage.

***

When Simon was back at the temporary expedition site codename 666.

She told him once he was leaving she was craving for him. Once her proud nation's leader was at home, she was far more aroused next door to him.

He reported His Excellency Blond's wife's words on the papers and took the night off early to plan tomorrow once Detective Simpleton approves planning permission.

While Yami and Nami were on their way to honour God's Bakura, wishes made at the altar avenged the innocence and fed her blood of demons.

***

Mage was in a morning navigating through plan setting the route of Vanguard to Simon, he taking the rearguard and leaving sideguard to Ignacius to oversee their rookies to freedom of our Bob and Dylan.

"It will not be as usual because our site is the walt to archives kept close to gold's deposit safe."

"It will be high guarded and armed because we are here and we killed making this Nation status to death communication 10, the top terrorism alert."

"But since we are not terrorists, we do not care. We aim and fire at them to stop pure evil from massacring the innocent world."

"Roger?"
They all screamed, "Copy That Commanding Officer Mage."

Godmorgan Era of Satan

They summoned the two hounds in Dark Castle. They wear leather and had a mission to guard his son Rudolf, the future impaler of sex, to threaten our seven heroes' futures.

While he was out to see his surroundings.

He left his castle for others to orgy he could show around his lands at night for his sex tool the Vikings had sent him. He loved his new playthings.

It chained them to the neck near toilets. The men the Dark Lord had made from honest politicians who opposed his sick laws.

He had them have sex with pigs and goats before they lost their sanity. He sexually abused their family members before they submitted themselves to pledge their loyalty for life in exchange to live another day.

Meanwhile, from outside the Dark Lord's castle, the slugs went through the young prince's chest while he was masturbating on the toilet seat.

"I think I got one prick."

"Those slugs are for those that courts won't judge, you better watch where you hit."

The demolition brothers Bob and Dylan were having a conversation behind sniper rifle optics.

Our vanguard was closing in by the castle moat to open the gates.

The time elite rearguard was watching sideguard wasting their slugs and counting ammunition to clear their path for entry to end this pure evil of Crimson Nation.

When it came in view of a depravity to vanguard enter castle's hall and see the Cabinet of Education ministers from Gothminster Palace having an orgy forcing young choir of girls from local boarding school in underage sex.

The Cabinet Ministers were forcing themselves on young girls wearing t-shirts written on them as King of Porn.

But Bob sneezes and opens fire through letter O of the cabinet minister' t-shirt, starting a scene from depravity to massacre.

"I hope this won't make trouble because the rearguard told us off already for last aimless fire."

The vanguard has nothing left but to control the situation and contribute to the first round of assault before they can let in the rearguard team waiting outside.

"I wonder what is happening from inside with all guns clapping."

"I think our guys got ambushed."

"Let's clear the bridge with grenades because we cannot confirm a positive ID."

"Sideguard, do you copy? You are open to aim and fire."

"Copy that."

When the rearguard enters the site, they flank our vanguard to a defensive corner waiting for the help because they blocked a radio signal with a transmitter blocking paint in the hall of orgy evil Dark Lord designed to keep his servants happy.

Commanding officer takes no time to open fire from his AK102 assault rifle aiming at a tactical reflective shield.

He aims below the view gap because bullets spin always upward and distance of the aim from metres determines in millimeters on his sight.

The first round goes below taking a second direct headshot at a hostile because he knows in such an exchange half a second determines if you stay alive and can carry on your assignment further.

He takes a further step to open the path for the trapped vanguard but he is held off by Dark Lord soldiers further off the hall next to colons, taking heavy fire round his shoulders in a cover.

Simon aims the feet of the last tactical shield foot soldier, making him fall down on his knees and he pushes the shield back, stepping on him to kill him through open gun fire on his face 10 centimetres apart off victims head.

When vanguard opens a clear path they move from hall to hall but are not able to find any presence of Dark Lord except the dead kid on the toilet seat before they force Simon to shoot dead two guys in dark Spandex suits with dog collars chained in front of the entrance.

They take a retreat from their target site. When Dark Lord returns from his full moon, walk in the surrounding forest and find his castle set ablaze, all captured on fire.

"Well my Viking lover we have no sex cave anymore."

"You do not worry, I want you to ride me anywhere you can."

***

Our Suki sisters are watching their evil site of evil on fire. When they notice men in black tactical unit uniforms returning to their vehicles after they cleared their den.

The sounds of a sniper rifle do not stop for a while before our twin sisters turn around and cancel tonight's plans they had made for the Dark Lord's castle.

"I wonder who were those men in daku?"

"I think some robber's gone home wrong."

"I like it."

"Why?"

"The robbery went south."

"Hahahaha."

But sisters laughing out loud went back to theirs government borrowed vehicle to scheme another way of finding to plot their murder plans further.

***

The time came for detective Simpleton to announce the course of change because he was in contact with local guilds who were working also in the background to eradicate Dark Lord's evil from their Island long ago they loved and killed for it.

Our hero Mage was going through planning in conversation to learn about new action points they take to rob the Bank of Sinners, making a point they would not tolerate aggression from the Crimson Lord.

"I think this goes beyond our imagination" Simon took a cup of morning coffee and walked away to see the sunrise.

"I do not believe we are imaging or this is reality. I cannot see beyond the point of reason fighting this mythical Lord who is the bringer of evil."

Mage takes his cup of coffee and joins Simon on the terrace overseeing the Lake view.

"I am in conversation with you. It is not NATO duty to oversee perverts and crooked politicians who are incapable of bringing war. I understand our unit duty is to prevent causes of war rather than become part of warfare."

"Yes, this guerilla conflict is to avoid civil war but they should take responsibility for what is their homeland rather than us."

Simon takes a last drink from his coffee cup and before he walks away to check on others, he says they are risking their lives here to the commanding officer.

***

The morning Suki sisters were having a full Crimson brunch in the local inn.

They booked a twin room before their next stop to investigate those strange men who did their best to rob them of their targets.

Aim and Fire

Ignacius was thinking to ask Simon if he remembers the story of someone who jailed them for double homicide but he relaxed into the sofa seat and he was thinking long before today.

They arrived at the location before their Captain Mage and had to run area checks to learn about local surroundings.

It was a hot and sunny summer's afternoon.

They went out to a local pub drinking and met two beautiful Dutch women sitting near the river with maxi dresses revealing their legs closer to torso.

"What are you doing in such heat in the sun?"

"I can see you are laughing and having a great time."

"Well, we are relaxing." The girls laughed when Simon opened the conversation.

The two friends took time off and showed their girls the good time.

But when the night came they woke up in their beds naked and the lovers for the night went missing

They left in the morning for a full lunch menu and noticed outside their cafe a police presence and lots of local people standing close.

Ignacius said to Simon he believes it is old plastic washed ashore and the local community gathered to clean it up but Simon asked Ignacius to stop joking and he walked towards the crowd.

When he realized the crime scene victims, he froze in fear, his heart stopped.

Ignacius walked closer to him and rested his arm on Simon's shoulder to see closer. "OMG, I cannot believe it is two loose Dutch women who had a great orgy last night!"

"We better walk away." But when Simon finished his sentence, the thoughts his DNA found in their dead bodies will make him a criminal for life, made him desperate to wish he runs but he knew they needed the real culprit.

"I think we have a serial killer on the loose."

"I am feeling sick in my heart knowing how much pleasure we had they gave us and now seeing these rotten corpses fished out the water."

Our heroes did little, they knew the reasoning behind two murders they felt victims for. They walked away and left the hotel room early, taking their bedsheets with them.

"I think we are going camping tonight."

"I hate those bugs around us when it gets dark."

"They are better than prison food I guarantee you."

When they found a local forest near the motorway with an old barn left behind without use, they felt it would be great shelter to set their tents in and to set fire burning for their hotel bedding and boil hot soup.

The soup was boiling, Ignacius threw in a couple potatoes to let flames steam off from inside.

"When I find those pricks, I give them some metal."

"How do you know it is them and they are males?"

"I am sure it is sick bastards who killed our good night focks." Simon pushed around fire wood with his stick to let it burn even.

"I am sure they would give me a double blow job by the fire if they were still breathing."

"You are sick, Ignacius. Do you know that?"

"I just love life and good living."

The very next morning the headlines in local Sinbury papers wrote about two men wanted for a rape and murder of two female victims.

Simon and Ignacius tried to flee the city, but they apprehended them when one driver reported two hitchhikers looking similar to the suspects from the image of hotel CCTV pictures.

They did not resist making an arrest nor declined their saliva swab test to match found in victims' bodies.

While in the holding cell, Simon was thinking long and hard about who could have made them fall for the crimes they did not commit. But when the note passed under his door saying they must run to learn the truth today.

Simon made a knock on the door and asked if he could use the toilet before he could have more tea.

When the police station officer turned the key and pulled the door open, Simon hit his head on the door, throwing him backwards.

He stepped out and hit the officer's head with his boot.

"I am sorry mate but it will hurt me more than you."

He took his keys and opened Ignacius' cell door, letting him out and passing a police issued rifle.

"What took you so long?"

"I wonder what took Mage so long to post us a letter?"

"I cannot answer the question but we have a positive ID of the killer and we are taking police transport."

The little serial killer knew he would meet tonight machine versus machine.

They parked a police car two streets down the killer's house and booted doors open killing serial rapists in a single headshot from the picture they found inside an envelope our Detective Simpleton handed them in a local park.

His brains and blood particles splattered all over his family on their dinner table.

The moment they showed up, they left their crime scene, leaving no traces behind them.

When all was done Ignacius got drunk on home made whisky and he felt he cannot handle the night any further. Police arrested them driving around a river in a stolen jet ski wearing blue suits and neckties over their heads screaming at local water-way police. "Banzai!"

The next day our heroes were trying on their prison uniforms.

Their Captain was at the right altitude and speed flying to a private airport. He mixed with the world's most famous rock band to work as equipment assistant.

In the night our Simon was in his prison cell and he was thinking to himself. "She felt so good on him riding reverse cowgirl saying Sliht to him."

Ignacius in the opposite cell thought to himself they will have to tattoo tear drops on their cheeks.

The very next morning Ignacius told Simon they assigned him the D911 number and Simon told him he was an A113 prisoner.

They had a week before the final court trial and had good lessons about prison life.

It felt a little odd in gothic built prison barracks separated with narrow corridors as they walked, all inmates looking at them as if they did something wrong. Knowing they were in for a rape and murder trial since they had no proof left. They felt guilty.

The morning Ignacius was having his morning shower in a steam-packed showeroom with four facets near the toilet seat off the entrance. He sprays water on the inmate taking his clothes off.

He took a moment to brush water off his eyes to look at Ignacius and then he told his friends to stand watch at the door.

He took his top off and from his sleeve a small razer in between his fingertips.

"Now you are focked mate."

The other guys captured D911 by his armpits, taking him naked to the walls while a hot shower sprayed.

He kicked his feet away but the strength of the grip over his shoulders was too strong. He shouted but one inmate closed his mouth with the palm of his hand.

Simon walked to have his morning shower with his new friends to learn the door is held closed.

"What is the plug, ladies?"

He kicked doors open enough to see they are attempting to cut his friend.

With little thinking he ran in and his group of friends too.

They grabbed the men attempting to block the doors by their shoulders and did wrestle them down below the waist to smack their skulls to the walls.

Simon rushed forward and kicked the guy in his back from off his way who held a prison weapon.

Men lost their concentration allowing Ignacius to set his right arm free to punch the guy on his left on stomach while he was not letting go of his arm.

Ignacius used his left arm to twist around the arm that was holding him and with a light hip twist he broke it to pieces.

He pushed them together and kicked both aside as they slipped on the soap covered floor knocking their breath out of their lungs creating a feeling they cannot breathe in.

"Are you ok?"

"This one is a nasty piece of shat!"

"Guys, hold the doors till I place him where he belongs!" Then Simon picked him off the floor by his neck and pulled him to the toilet seat.

"I was only teaching our rookie a lesson."

Simon took no time listening to him beg for mercy and flipped him overhead, drowning his head in the toilet feces.

"I think your foul mouth belongs here." Simon was thinking while he was gasping for air in the dirt.

***

When Ignacius finished telling his prison story it amazed Mage about their prison school.

"It sounds a little like a life Ignacius."

"I would not call it but it was like no other experience I felt."

"You guys try easy next time and no slapping random asses while on a mission no matter how much honey you think you will find inside."

"Yes, the sex was great but who could tell it was a serial psychopath who did kill them after the girls left our bedroom before their morning flight."

"You should keep your battleship mast to yourself. We focus on mission we could go home and then maybe I let you have some because you and Simon are like sex addicts."

Simon walks with a smile. "We may be addicts but who loves a good possy they can find."

Their conversation stops when our Detective Simpleton is reporting good news.

Do you like Koto flavour?

The morning Dark Lord was drinking his coffee he leaned on his chair and was looking through Dark Castle out in blue skies.

The one faithful morning he remembers his youth how he and his schoolmates visited His Excellency Blond's home.

They were school friends who were upper classmates to young Blond. They saw Blond in his house and they played games on his game station.

His friends were sitting in the lounge shouting and running across fields of mushrooms in a video game attempting to avoid obstacles to save the princess in time he said he needed to take a leak.

Young Blond was sitting in a corner feeling isolated from his school friends with dark eyelids from school work.

Dark Lord walks in a corridor and walks towards the restroom to see a divorced homemaker preparing snacks for her son's upperclassmen.

Young Lord looks at her and feels the temptation to have the desert she has early.

He walks up to her and places his arm down her waist with others squeezing her butt.

"Did your Mr. Blond leaves you because you are not good enough to look after his rejects?"

She speaks nothing but licks her lips and concentrates, completing her dessert.

He feels more tempted to open her up for no reason and pushes her waist closer to the kitchen top where she is standing.

He rubs his groin closer to her and pulls her top down halfway, revealing her chest and bra she is wearing.

"I told you in the name of my royal household to kneel before me and beg for redemption you give me."

She kneels on her knees with her hands shaking in panic to avoid any trouble with her son because her husband abandoned them long ago they cannot afford the trouble.

He spits down the sink and tells her to open his zip and let her know what she will need to do next so she could serve her country.

She strokes her hand down his waist and takes out the young Dark Lord's pride and joy, stroking it a couple times before she places it in her mouth.

When upperclassmen get tired and leave a joystick to another kid, he could see what desert is taking so long he walks in the kitchen seeing his country's future lord spreading open a homemaker on the kitchen counter top.

Her legs open and wrapped around his Dark Lord, keeping her mouth shut and kissing his neck with her plain gaze at his classmate.

"I will finish it soon, there is nothing to stare at."

The Dark Lord tells another kid who continues walking in the restroom to look in a mirror, pick between his teeth and check his breath after he spits in the sink.

He walks out and he can see the young Dark Lord finished spreading his seed between her.

His classmate walks up to her and asks his Dark Lord to play console in another room because the pause will not last long.

He decided he had not done it from behind yet and would like to practice it while she is fit for it.

He pulls her arm and tells her to bend over. He could see her taking off her underwear. He could observe her cleaning the fluids dripping from her with it he could be sure the passage is clean enough to start over.

She does as he says and when children are done playing, they wish good bye to each other thanking for hospitality waves goodbye before leaving the household.

***

When our Mage had a positive message over concealed radio transmission from Mr. Simpleton, they left early in the morning to seek justice for the island they sought to leave.

They drove in black four wheel drive car made bulletproof pass buildings made a century ago but avoided world war bombs.

They were checking their assault rifles for cartridges and counting bullets before the eventual destination.

Mage was thinking to himself why Detective Simpleton told him to leave Dark Lord to be because four archangels said to him they will open seven gates under heaven to break the seal they kept locked from us and heaven itself the justice serves.

He thought the reasoning is unusual and why some sort of force should be able to devour the belly of the beast because the Blond or Dark Lord has an appetite for pure insanity of evil but who could cut them dead so easily.

With little time to think they reached their site and Simon drove up the stairs, the Bank of Sinisters forcing passersby to run to the side watching black SUV forcing its way to the Nation's Bank.

Simon jumped outside, but he was not wearing his black Swiss style tactical gear. He was wearing royal crimson family attire with a printed paper mask of the Dark Lord, the same dress code applied to Mage and Ignacius. When passersby thought they charged their own national bank shooting live rounds in bank security in front of them.

They did wear medals and royal crests it was difficult to say it was not the royal crimson family taking up violence on the street.

The team charged the Bank of Sinisters, shooting security guards down, avoiding leaving anybody breathing able to use firearms.

They hit the blond lady's head over the counter because she was too slow to tell them where the key to the safe was.

Simon took his handgun and forced her throat, explaining to her he will shoot it better than from his testicles.

She had a tear in her eyes and pointed her finger to the draw where they found the vault master key.

Simon said thank you to the blond lady. "We will fock later once I cash my check in darling."

Our heroes were taking a corridor to the vault when Simon saw passing him by a Bank Manager with his name badge saying Carl Pirdila.

He made a roundhouse kick and cracked his skull to the wall.

"Take this satanic manager."

When our heroes run outside holding top secret government documents, money, crown jewelry and digital stock market keys plus a couple gold bars, they realize they are surrounded by an incoming police force.

The boot of their black SUV opened over seeing police vehicles towards them but the grandmother who looked alike stood up pushing her tired hairy leg out of the boot wearing a royal family dress.

She stood up, looking at speeding police vehicles towards her, gave a good stretch to her back from side to side and picked up her rocket launcher.

She took the safety lid off, aimed and fired at police carnage of transport.

Around the corner a white van started its engine and with screeching wheels made a round turn from the parking space.

Two window cleaners from the van opened their side doors with the big motto logo We Clean it for U, ahead of the burning and tilted police transport and waved their hands at our heroes.

The cosplay of the royal family ran inside their transport and drove off.

"Blast, this skirt waist is not mine." He pulled the paper mask off and opened a bottle of lager.

"Yes Detective Simpleton, I think skirts and dresses never suited you."

They all laughed.

"But I am sure I gave them a big one."

Once they lost their stolen transport, they sat in Detectives Simpleton's wide car and drove to a pub called Pig Pit to have their well deserved drinks.

After a few drinks they meet a couple cute girls talking about Disco down the road from where they are.

"Oh, you are Detective Mr. Simpleton. We are sure we will meet one."

Two cute Japanese girls laughed.

"What a coincidence, we were planning to cut our business trip short before we head back home to Japan but I think we are ok to have a delightful dance."

"I am sure my nephews would be more than happy to escort you."

Our Detective Simpleton pours the last pint of lager to his mouth and leaves home to watch tomorrow's news about four archangels promised they sent from the heavens to save our earth.

Bob and Dylan were standing in the corner and smiling at our young heroes, thinking they would meet excellent partners for tonight.

They waved their hands, smiling.

"Good luck lads! We think we will stay here for a few more drinks before we crawl back to our beds."

Ignacius walks to two girls to say he learned about them from his uncle Simpleton.

"I think my uncle said we are free to escort you to the disco tonight in case there are no good dance partners."

"Yeh, I think he mentioned something."

Nami looks at her sister and smiles, who is looking at their drinks menu.

Simon is so drunk he stumbles on Ignacius' shoulder, holding a cocktail of whiskey and energy drink, looking to learn the conversation.

"We must enjoy tonight because stargazing told me it is the right tonight."

Our girls laughed and offered him a few more drinks before they would see him fit, have them out on a date tonight.

"Ok, guys, you know what I told you about drinking and dating beautiful women?"

"Roger that, Captain Crimson, but we're done for tonight?"

"Yeah, it is true and I think I am ok to see you out of this pub before you vomit here."

They left for the dance floor to see a guest DJ Kuku Kola.

The place was so great and music was swinging the atmosphere well they started dancing under the disco floor.

"I think this tune beats harder than a police officer when you are drunk on the floor."

"I think this beats harder than grandmother's pain killers."

"No! I think it beats harder than a drunk father from the bar."

"Nope. It beats harder than pandemia."

Do you say Sakai?

The team loaded their assault rifles and wore full assault gear Simon Says said to them before the last mission together.

"Tonight we load some timber and it will be tonight they will remember."

The team left seeking revenge for the entire nation with only two faithful nationals who escaped their prison.

Our Detective Simpleton was home relaxing because he knew it would shake the nation about justice served before Crimson King and his country were taken for ransom.

"You hear us guys, we take no prisoners and kiss them hard with our slugs."

"Yes, we fock them hard like our first and last love."

"Roger, we closed our radio channel. We start work."

The Tvart Way 10 had an urgent office meeting they called Snake, where all official heads of government had to complete strategic planning to resolve the crisis their nation experienced after their Bank of Sinisters lost state secrets, including valuable assets.

The time outside our Bob and Dylan the Demolition Brothers cut the throats of a couple police officers standing guard at the rear post.

"We are like a couple cut throats."

"Yeh and a very low rent."

Meanwhile, once blood did not finish leaking out officers' throats, the major assault team made their way to the main entrance because time was the key to essence in operation the Black Edge they were preparing in the former abandoned military facility the Black Site.

Once they stormed into the building, Bob dropped a bag of plastic explosions close to the electric generator for the team captain to detonate it and turn off the power supply, creating a blackout.

When they opened the last door and murdered the last guards, they shot dead all the secretaries of Crimson state.

"What do we do with this woman?"

Simon Says without further talk fired two slugs in His Excellency Blond chest.

"You give her a good fock."

When Mage walks in to inform he has secured the escape route perimeter, he can see Simon sitting in the highest ranked government officials chair smoking a cigar. Ignacius is pumping his mast through the open zip in His Excellency wife between her spread while she is rubbing her arms on his flag vest and kissing his neck.

"You guys make me sick every time I let you take control."

He splashes her blood and part of brains over Ignacius' face.

"I was about to do her in. Simon said she is a great joy ride."

"Well, I finished for you. You can close your zipper or if you love corpses go ahead while we head home."

He stood up, zipped his crotch and spat down. "I think we are done here."

Simon places his cigar and picks up his CAR 15 make rifle.

"She was just a joy ride, let's move on, brothers. We need a real future to catch."

"I would rather live a moment than think anything is greater."

"Well said Ignacius."

"Thank you, our Captain."

He saluted our Mage. And they took an escape route to take cover and lie low before Detective four archangels will make a miracle they were waiting for.

***

The Dark Lord in his Dark Castle just finished his phone call listening to his kingdom politicians getting murdered by well prepared assailants with unknown origins to the police force.

He places his phone down and takes a deep breath, letting his air out, and closes his eyes.

"At least Blond slat made me two kids."

He opens his mini bar and takes a bottle of rum to celebrate the dead weak and strong who will survive.

But it felt like time had stopped and the Deja Vu moment made him think something was not right.

He can see dark smoke coming from all gaps of windows and doors, making his hand shake, feeling faint legs.

He cannot move or scream at his guard to save him from fire to learn now in the middle of his dark hall is a standing black figure in dark steel armour looking at him.

"You are the one who calls himself the supreme commander?" The hard voice spoke to him.

But before Dark Lord of Crimson Nation could open his jaw to let sound out.

'I see you are a weakling not worth your titles nor life you. Die."

Grand Duke, who traveled from stones of time in his sleep from the illustrious past of Grand Duke's Kingdom, closed his arm the moment he spelled Die.

He left the Dark Lord a splatter of blood covering every corner of Crimson Nation Dark Hall.

***

The very next morning the young Viking Princess was packing her bags to take the first flight back home and on the table were the Morning Nation newspaper.

The headlines were about acts of terrorism taking lives of innocent His Excellency family and his government secretaries suspects related to the day before armed robbery of the National Bank. With most shocking news our Crimson Lord turns ill and became diseased, medics confirmed morning after act of terrorism.

She just packed her bags and took black taxi to a major airport because she felt there was no more fun to play with in her desires.

She thought on her way to the airport which nation's lord would be great next sex toy.

The taxi driver packed her luggage on a trolley, and she paid him a tip.

She looked at boarding time and walked to powder her makeup fresh before she boarded her business class seat back to Viking Kingdom.

The ladies' lounge restrooms were clean and full of fresh odour, to see an oriental girl cleaning toilet seats. She felt disgusted that she was sucking on her candy in her lips while brushing the floor.

"Could you leave, I prefer private time in the ladies room."

"Apologies." She made a light bow and started walking away.

"But you die." Nami said and spit in her neck vocal cords light poison needle.

Yami walked out from the occupied cabin and closed her mouth with tissue pulling her inside.

The time came a few hours later for her driver to pick his Princess but he learned she did not board her flight back home, he found only her luggage sent home.

But when he picked up her luggage, the airport guard dog started barking at him and security had to open her bags, finder her cut in pieces covered in plastic.

Yami and Nami landed in the same flight watching how their faces turned pale watching a scene from a horror movie.

"They can build her back to a stone statue."

"Yep. It will last longer than her sick desires to fock every nobleman she can find."

They took a taxi and continued to their hotel to close their business deal.

***

Mage and his team were giving their last goodbyes before they boarded the fishing boat, taking them back to safety after their hardship completing their mission they got from Detective Simpleton.

Bob and Dylan were standing tall and firm, proud after participating in NATO Black Site camp training helped them assist seasoned soldiers in combat operations.

"We learned so much from you, Simon. The lessons we took on how to use sharps and how to keep it. We are happy you advised us and trained how to store poison on your sleeve the time we need it oiled on blades we use to make an escape."

"No worries lads. I was happy you learned rather than rot in Crimson Prison."

"Ok. We're done talking, the time is for us to go."

But out of nowhere Simon's feet began to smoke in black smoke engulfing him in black fire and dark clouds covered in black rain pulling Simon out of space through a black narrow corridor he can hear medical equipment beeping and feeling faint light coming through eyelids.

Korean Peninsula

Audrius Razma

"Only our children will know the truth."

-The Real Man

Secta

Simon wakes up from hospital bed in the northern side of peninsula border to see his teammates under oxygen and life support machines overseen by the Korean nurses.

He says to himself I cannot believe the dream.

"It was my late father taking me out of the darkness, his face was covered in scars and he was asking me to wake up."

"I still can hear his voice, wake up my son."

***

But before all came to a chance come to light we can follow our heroes journey.

Before she managed to arrive Simon Says went to a gym center and inside he entered a martial arts dojo for his first free lesson. He changed to black tracksuit bottoms and white t-shirt; he thought good sweat will help him avoid a stronger hangover.

Then he did ask for extra lessons to test his skills further because the group was for beginners. When he was training in private sparring the dojo master hit him in his back with bamboo straw to help him fight further, "attack attack", but he beat them up and bent them over their heads for apology suddenly to learn he broke a straw stick in a half and stuff it their backsides.

"Banzai!!!"

He was shouting and after he went out for cigarette leaving his new sensei suffer in dojo.

He drew on his hand three circles elongating middle one.

"I think it will be perfect Ikigai to them."

Later he in police custody while interrogated was asked what it is, and he replied, "it is my dick I whip you with".

He jabbed the station officer down to the floor and grabbed the running sergeant by his collar to smash his head so hard into the wall his hat fell off.

Now he has them tied down on the floor he starts kicking them and continues his investigation about the missing kid.

When Simon returns Ignacius asks him.

"How is their strong arm of the law?"

Simon drops his gym bag and before walks away he says, "They are still probably deeply in shat."

***

They welcome her into the Hansun apartment residency they rented for a couple days to complete the mission they were given.

She steps in the lift giving a shy smile to see Simon smiling full cheeks back. Ignacius winks at her and Mage keeps a close eye on her and then exchange expressions.

They walk in through the apartment door and Simon says to her he will personally show her room so she could settle in as quickly as possible and while she puts the bags down, he would make her cup of black coffee.

When she walks away.

Mage is holding his mobile phone in hand looking at the message, he just received.

Simon look at him while he is boiling the kettle he says, "I would love to have one of those super phones but my budget cannot allow it", Mage "we keep minimal contacts with the boss therefore we keep limited connection devices in our team."

Simon, "What is good online for us to know?"

Mage sits down, closes the phone and leans his head back to close his eyes.

"It is nothing much in our network, it just report came in the BBD Brit secret service has one gone missing after he decided to accept murder contract and kill one well known boxer. I think the agent 's name is Edward Hogson."

Simon pours in hot water for coffee to brew and places one cup close Mage.

"I think I was watching the news other day and they mention some sort of murder investigation."

Then Mage picks up the cup of coffee and starts walking to the end of the corridor, "I will take her coffee to her to see how she is doing and do not forget our codenames we only use because she has her own we do not know."

Simon, "Roger that and over or out", then he places his legs on the table and has his fifth cup of strong coffee today.

Mage walks up to her bedroom and gives a knock to her door, "Sakura-san it is Algimant-senpai and I am holding your coffee."

She opens her door, "arigato".

She uses her both hands to take coffee from him, "I would like to know where the washroom is because Vlad-senpai was so urgent I would see my bedroom. I was not able to know the apartment well."

He shows her around the penthouse suite apartment then he smiles.

"Apologies we were on low funds to have it with a swimming pool." She smiles too.

When she did have her hot shower, the guys were preparing a strategic team meeting and was completing data analysis of geographic and cultural objectives.

She walks in blue jeans white silk shirt and says she is happy to have the work done together.

"I am happy we can work together and I would like to be debriefed how much we are making progress in our case".

Team captain Mage looks across the living room dining table and says to her she could join a spare seat to join the data analysis.

"We have a belief it is an organized local crime syndicate responsible for kidnapping our target and they are be believed to make an attempt to ask a ransom in later date but we have no such time left to conclude therefore we are made to act in such quick way."

Sakura sits down and looks through Daily Bong newspapers archives the team had received from the data analysis team after their field Intel was complete.

"I see Aisel Hasel Goon and Sin On are the top suspects to be masterminds in the conflict to come."

Simon grabs a bit of his lunch sandwich and once he swallows with a cup of water, he takes another copy of the report they had received and pushes across the table to her.

"I think tonight we can raid their nightclub the Iron Quest to see if we can make vital intel points for us to complete on time."

Ignacius brushes his right arm across his brown beard.

"We are the Littland Organized Crime Group we have portrayed the other night and we should press the overseas mafia's attempts to have the race for control of the country."

Sakura looks to Ignacius, "How we proceed."

Ignacius, "we made clear the fictional crime boss and his henchman identity, for us to conclude Vlad is Jon Gi Sigis and Sin On is just a ghost to cause larger distortion."

Mage concludes the team meeting.

"Great, welcome to the northern European mind games, I hope you will like it."

Sakura stands up and makes a short bow.

"Arigato."

Mage suddenly stops to stand up,.

"My apologies, I almost forgot our communication codenames because we use

pseudonyms while we work but we will need open channel names. I was instructed to inform you I am Live Wire, Vlad is Torpedo, Pioter is The Streets and Sakura is Wildflower."

***

While the daybreak was near the end and night life slowly creeps in the day, the NBL special delivery courier pulls over the back door to deliver the package addressed to Sin On.

The delivery man walks out the driver seat to open rear van door looking down the floor and walks to intercom to dial the doorbell call.

"I have a special delivery for mister Sin On therefore I would be happy to have him to sign the parcel today."

Chapter 1

Then couple minutes later you can hear the steps taken leading down from office above the ground floor storage gate when delivery man picks up the metal bar near waste container and breaks down security camera; then man opens quickly the door inside grey gates for Simon to spray in Sin On face.

"I hate bad breath", when man quickly collapses Simon throws in the parcel and pulls in Sin On inside the van to escape.

Mage parked the blue van near the district the team was taken to enjoy nightlife the previous day by their new acquaintance Bibi Bit.

"I think Sakura-san, you had a great strategy for us just to locate the important target rather than causing a mess and waste of time clearing their night club."

Sakura was sitting inside the van with Ignacius and was talking about planning and concluding the post-intel action plan how they could proceed the rescue when radio makes a spark and they can hear Simon.

"The Torpedo has completed it and now heading towards The streets assembly plan."

When they hear loud vibrating sound after they start their vehicle.

Simon starts his van in a hurry and when he runs the speeding vehicle down the corner he presses the remote inside his pocket to cause a large explosion from a parcel he threw inside the nightclub back gates.

When he stops in the outskirts of Seoul in an old abandoned road around the corner from the cargo container, he radios through to Mage.

"The Torpedo has delivered a patient to the care home."

Mage opens the door of the shipping container.

"The visiting tour has just started."

They open the van doors and cover his head with a coffee bean bag then they gently lift him out the van holding onto his arms and legs carrying him inside the container to place him onto a chair.

Sakura uses rope around his legs and finishing the knot around his waist.

Simon pulls out a small jab needle and injects it in his neck. Ignacius leans back at the side of the container and looks in the direction the sun is setting down.

"Do you think it will work?"

Simon places the lid back on the needle and takes it back into his pocket.

"I am sure it will work Pioter, do you remember when I passed out during our mountain trek training and the big boss brought me back to life with the same chemical to complete the last 10 kilometers run with 20 kilograms bags over our shoulder?"

When Sin On starts to move his head and increases his breathing.

Mage without waiting a moment to see how he responds to adrenaline, pulls the bag over Sin On's head and shows him a picture of their mission target.

"Do you know this kid?"

Sin On opens one eye. "Why should I tell you anything!" Then Simon slaps him over his face. "I think you should learn manners before we make you speak."

Sin On takes a good look at Simon and spits on his shoe after Ignacius walks in. "I think we finished here, I just opened his mobile encryption and synchronized his GPS history data to conclude we are dealing with a kidnapper."

Sakura Uto without taking a second longer pulls out her small silver open and presses it twice open to stab Sin On in the neck.

Simon takes a look at her small clenched fist with a silver pen sticking out of it, "What a nice middle finger she has."

Mage start to take the ropes down and asks his team to help him to carry Sin On out the container.

They walk around the side of the container near a large hole they dig inside the ground, they place the Sin On unconscious on to the ground and Simon pushes him with his foot inside.

"I think you guys was doing a lot of labor while I was driving around club district.".

Mage takes a shovel and starts to throw the soil back into the pit, Ignacius walks up the pile of rocks piled up right next to the shovel and picks one up.

Mage asks Ignacius to stop with the huge rock in his hand.

"We must wait before he has white foam out his mouth to know the black crab poison is effective."

The moment he says about the poison the moment white foam start to float out Sin On's mouth but suddenly Ignacius throws the large rock on to his head making blood splatter over the ground.

Simon, "I was hoping you will not make me puke today Pioter".

Ignacius, "I just relieved his pain and misery although I know his nerves had gone numb three seconds after he had it but just in case."

Simon, "I think you have problems Pioter".

Mage, "No complaining and we all start pouring the soil back in."

When they finish with the shovels, they take off the overalls and place them in a bin bag, and then hop in their black SUV.

Mage, "I hope we all are happy with our nature sightseeing today?"

Simon, "Yay it was fun fact."

Sakura, "I named my weapon a little finger."

Simon, "I wonder how about us?"

Ignacius leans back in the leather passenger seat, "I would like to call my knife a War Saber."

Simon, "I know all about your walking stick saber."

He starts to laugh and before he finishes laughing Mage interrupts.

"I would call my handgun Daku, because I like to know I can carry at ease inside my jacket and I like it black."

Simon, "I would never think about naming a dead thing with the name but if you guys talk about the fighting spirit, I could have it named a Whistle."

Mage, "How would you justify it?"

Simon, "I think at the times when we did not have real technology, a police whistle was the only way to announce the crimes."

They start their Black SUV and drive off the bumpy ride across into a clear narrow road leading back to the capital.

When they park back at the Hansun Apartments Mage tells them, he will return the SUV and on the way back he will complete the report back to NATO Vice-Commander about today.

He steps out of his taxi and when walks in the apartment lounge he sits down in the one seat sofa, places his left arm at the wooden arm of the chair and comfortably places his spine in soft black leather.

He opens his mobile screen and sends a message in a dating app X-partner a message to girl.

"I think a lot about you and I made arrangements for us to go out on a date, my work is fine so far and I think I finish on time for a meeting at the cinema in two days."

Then a message comes back in X-partner, "I am happy to hear from you. I look forward to our lovely evening together."

Then he stands up and walks towards the lift, he opens the lift door with the resident card and walks in pressing the top floor button.

He comes back everyone relaxing on the sofa in silence, with their eyes closed like they would seek meditation relief.

"I never thought you guys are doing group nirvana seeking."

Simon turns his head, "I never did but I just enjoy a moment of silence."

Mage walks in to his bedroom and takes a fresh towel before he goes in a hot shower.

When they all had a good shower they were enjoying a cold bottle of water and relaxing in silence inside the living room on a large sofa.

Simon, "I think we know a very great tour operator around here."

The doorbell rings and when Ignacius opens the door Bibi Bit is standing outside smiling.

Ignacius asks him to wait for them to get ready in 30 minutes and they will meet across the street in residential gardens.

Simon walks in his room to look for a blue t-shirt with a grey shiny suit he bought from a street merchants tailor shop in Bangkok.

Mage puts on a grey t-shirt and brown slim linen suit and Ignacius pulls out his suitcase white t-shirt and soft cotton blue suit.

Sakura walks in her bedroom and changes to black silk underwear and bra. She looks for her grey cotton maxi dress, brown sandals and takes her black evening bag she is holding inside black pouch, her folding mobile, the top designer watch 'travel machine' and her flower scent perfume she sprays two times around her before she takes white band to place her hair together.

She takes a look in a mirror and is thinking she is cute already to go out with new friends.

When they close the apartment and take the elevator to the ground entrance into the hall Simon offers to give her his arm so she could feel comfortable walking out.

They walk through the lounge of the entrance with brown sofa chairs and silver marble floor through the facade of exotic flowers and through a glass entrance into the path leading across the car park in residential gardens.

Militant Wifo

Simon whispers to her ear, "Do not worry about our yayaya or ahh. You are perfectly good enough for us."

Bibi Bit starts to wave at them when he throws his cigarette and starts to smile.

Bibi Bit takes his phone out and makes a quick phone call before he meets the team.

"I just made a taxi call for all of us. I also was not aware you guys are four now. I am lucky enough I ordered large enough transport to fit us all in tonight."

Simon, "Ya."

Bibi Bit has a close look at their attractive companion, "Hello, I am Bibi Bit and I am happy to meet you."

Sakura makes a quick bow, "I am Sakura Uto, I am their business assistant to complete their business contract during their duration in Asia."

Bibi Bit smiles, "Ahh. I see you are from Japan. I am Korean myself but my father is Thai making me Korean Thai." Sakura, "I am happy to meet you."

***

They sit down in VIP corner table area and Bibi Bit mobile phone rings.

"Ok I see.", he covers his phone with his hand, "Apologies but I forgot to order next week stock for café place I work for therefore I go out just have a moment to see what I might need for the weekend delivery I could open next week."

Simon is looking at the menu, "No worries Bit, we start drinks without you."

When Bibi Bit is absent Ignacius has two shots.

"Here is for Littland! Kanpai!" He places some cash on the waitress tray before she walks away, and she smiles.

He clears the throat after two double shots of strong spirit with soda water and then he picks up Sakura hand, "Let's all go out on the dance floor to have fun."

Sakura is smiling and listening with her eyes close to enjoy the music, "The DJ Kooka Kolla is mixing great tonight."

Ignacius, "Who is that Kooka Kolla you talking about."

Simon makes a quick turn around, "Now look at her, the whole club looking at her."

When they take a break from the dance floor the guys decide to go out for a cigarette and Sakura politely declines because she never did smoke and does not like the smell.

When Ignacius is walking waving his hand and enjoying the environment he accidentally touches a man in a black suit wearing a white shirt with an open collar and he looks into his face he grabs Simons should, "waaait it is our brother Jack...",

Simon quickly grabs Ignacius to pull him and make him walk forward the exit, "I do not have time for your brother Jack, I am craving for a smoke"

When they reach the exit the door attendants politely asks them to go to the side smoking area and when they walk to the empty smoking area they suddenly experience electric shock from security guards who show them the way. They have cotton bags covered over their heads before they are pulled back into the nightclub storage room through emergency exit doors.

They kneel them on the floor in front of the camera and tell them to brush their palms in the camera begging for mercy.

When Sakura is sitting by herself and she thinks something is not right tonight and the barman points her three fellows to a security guard, it did seem awkward before they left.

She took a look in her black soft sheepskin leather evening bag made by Bersache for her mobile phone. When she took her mobile device out she opened the Team Point monitoring app unlocking it with her thumbprint and she can see them on a navigation map entering quickly back into the venue but she cannot see anyone coming in from the VIP lounge is waiting for them.

She takes her to leave to WC and as she walks in the restroom she locks the door behind her and takes another look in her Bersache bag.

She quickly finds a small black Bento box wrapped in a black velvet cloth, she takes out from the box a small-calibre handgun and a gun suspender she screws on.

Our Sakura double-checks her firearm before she loads the bullets into the cartridge.

Miss Uto leaves the WC area and starts walking in the direction of the storage room past the bathroom area leading down the basement stairs.

When she turns left she takes out her handgun walking down the stairs and walks holding it pressed down her black dress. It takes not much time before she comes to the restricted area door with an overweight man standing in front of the door.

"Konnichiwa, me bathroom, please"

The man places his hand in front of her stopping her and points his face with his gaze towards the back to stairs ordering her to leave the basement floor.

She smiles once and takes a bow gesture showing apology but she drops her bag and when she is reaching to pick up her handbag off the floor close to the man's feet, she hits him in the stomach with the handle of her gun.

When he gasps for air she hits him once more in his neck and smacks her knee in his mouth holding his face between her knee and metal frame door until he dies within a couple of minutes from an internal bleeding injury she caused with her handgun.

She takes off the ID card of his waist and uses it to unlock the metal-framed door with magnetic touch on his staff ID.

Once the door opens she points the gun forward, closing her left eye and making faster steps in the grey basement corridor.

She is walking faster, counting her concentration breath and keeping her eye at the point-blank end of her gun.

The gun was custom made and has no manufacturer's name making it harder to trace back, before she left Japan she had it posted in parts to many delivery centres in South Korea, including custom made lethal bullets allowing pierce bulletproof vests.

She is walking down the corridor and she can hear loud voices coming from the left door in the middle of the corridor when she can see a barman walking out from her right-hand side carrying a box of drinks from the storeroom.

She takes her aim and she can see when she presses the trigger, the hammer smashes back and blood drops backwards out of the barman´s head.

The shot knocks him back to the doorway making a bullet hole in his forehead, leaving blood drops splashed along the way.

He fell within a spare of the moment sliding down along the wall, still holding well onto the box of drinks he did carry while he was alive.

She continues walking forward past the dead body and without checking if the door handle is locked she uses her hard heel shoes to kick open the door handle and fires three more shots shooting down the cameraman and man holding Ignacius face.

She then kicks the waitress holding large pliers, "Koto kotato, thank you bitch bitch die die is perfectly honest enough for you."

Sakura takes a step back and fires a headshot for three friends to watch how waitress blood is dropping back off her skull on the floor.

Simon swallows down his dry throat and takes a look at Sakura.

"Oho."

Sakura, "We all are like this but those who survive are the ones who are faster enough to press the trigger."

She places her handgun back in Bersache handbag she bought last year in Kyoto.

"I am sorry I forgot to mention my second best friend is my Night Shadow."

Simon smiles and tries to stand up by his knees.

"I like her too with suspender," he smiles and stands up to brush the dust off his knees.

Sakura, "Now give a quick goodbye to the camera crew and let's head out."

She presses her two hands together and makes a quick bow.

"Let their spirits have some peace now."

She helps Ignacius with his hands tied down. "I think they were planning to murder you last." Mage stands up, "where you learned this kind of stuff", and then he kicks the camera tripod down.

Sakura replies, "I was gifted to stay with my grandfather after the rest of my family passed away."

Simon, "But how did they get my well-tailored Indian suit dirty", then he kicks the cameraman's dead body in his head.

Dogs of War

While Sakura had taken a look around through the back door Simon walked to a black van driver who was in garage alley road and was waiting for night club back doors to open so he could deliver three dead bodies to the dumping site.

Simon taps the man on his shoulder. "I think you are looking for me?".

He throws his fist to the man's face but he only manages to hit the end of his cigarette bit and Simon blows does not stop. He finished him hard with his elbow.

Simon picks the man on his black shirt collar and hits him on his neck with his left palm.

He quickly turns him round and hits the man's head with his knee into the wheel's rim leaving him lifeless.

Then Simon grabs the keys from his pocket and opens the back of the van door for rest to jump in.

"I think we have free wheels for tonight guys."

They leave to drive along the river Han and drive across the bridge in a car park near by Local Park overseeing the city lights. They sit on a bench waiting for Simon to clear off the vehicle.

When he comes back he carries with him a box of Soju.

"When I was looking in the back of their van I discovered it was a delivery van for the night club. We just busted."

He shakes the box full of Korean spirits and passes one each.

"What was all about Koto kototo?" Simon asks her.

Sakura takes one bottle from Simon of Soju.

"Arigato".

"I am from a small mountain village north of Hokkaido."

Sakura replies. "We do not feel comfortable repeating the same twice".

Simon places the box of drinks down and sits on it.

"I do not say even once when it comes to blasting the brains of others out."

He smiles and pours a drink down his throat.

Ignacius unscrews the lid of the glass bottle and takes a look at Sakura.

"I thought only bandits were from the mountains, at least they say in Japan".

Sakura starts to laugh.

"I think you know a lot about Japan, have you ever visited?"

Ignacius, "We all three were together in Japan."

Sakura, "What did you guys do in Japan?"

Simon, "We just spent our time in clubs and girls doing hydraulics making it bounce"

Sakura, "a?"

"Do not worry about them too much. We better take a look at the night sky, it is great for stargazing tonight from this spot."

Mage continues looking above him.

The night sky was bright with a full moon and shades of dark blue allowing to see all the stars and making them think how many are there.

***

The Korean Daily Bong newspaper has written an article about an incident that took place last night police reported about a gunfight in the night life Seoul district.

Simon picks up an international edition copy on the newsstand.

"I think our young gun is well known now."

Mage takes his eyes off his mobile phone.

"We are closing our rearguard from V formation to sharp arrow, it came just now from the Vice-Commander."

Simon places the piece of paper down.

"Are we now cutting the belly of the beast?"

Mage folds his mobile in half. "The time is running out and we need to finish it soon, let the others know we are pressing the investigation."

***

The next morning Ignacius walks in the office's facility wearing cleaners overalls and takes a lift to the third floor with a mop trolley.

He walks in the accountant department and starts to take the rubbish out and watches how the men are sitting in the morning briefing room.

He walks to one of the computers and opens it with a small screwdriver then removes the hard disk from the area in the manager's desk.

When the men in the briefing room office workers finish their coffee and stand up to leave.

Ignacius starts mopping the floor towards their door and when they open their door he turns his back to them.

Our Ignacius is holding a custom mop end he in particular did in order to be fitted half cut and empty inside placed with a 25 cm Japanese steel blade near the top of the handle.

He pulls out the hidden dagger and when he turns he slices the man's neck open with his right hand.

He kicks him, making the second target slip and fall with his dead friend.

He walks a few steps closer and swings his blade a couple times, making manager to dodge Ignacius blows but he suddenly reaches the end of the wall and his assistant is already facing the wall.

Ignacius kicks him in the stomach making them collide.

He pierces both of their necks with a sharp stab from top of their right neck down their lungs.

Quickly walks out and throws a bucket of floor bleach on the dead bodies in the briefing room.

He pulls in the hand of his blade inside the mop end and starts walking near the fire exit.

"Right now I just need to wipe off my blade."

He hears a sound near the staff room kitchen area and stabs through plastic glass piercing the secretary's soft small jaw and pulls down to the right side, slicing half of her jaw off cutting the plastic window down.

"She was cute."

Then trusts the blade right splashing remaining blood off and places on his left arm inspecting any minor dents to it.

He places it in his concealed mop end and walks out through the fire exit to the main service staff entrance and out the back door.

Ignacius closes his eyes in A15 public transport.

He is softly swaying side to side and A15 is making a humming sound to his ears.

"I wonder how others are doing and how Mage manages to do it for so long."

He is stretching his neck backwards to alleviate his fatigue.

Ignacius was wearing white t-shirt and blue jeans when he took off cleaning uniform. The neck on his shoulders are easing off.

He is relaxing his palms further holding his backpack in the passenger's seat.

He falls asleep dreaming sending Sakura messages until she gives in to him having an orgy but Sakura with her girlfriends was pushing him up and down while he is on top of her using her knees.

When he finished she said she liked his show and she passed him to another girl for kiss him while sweet talking him.

She oiled his condom, she climbed on top of him and pushed Ignacius inside for her to swing slowly side to side.

When she pulls him out of her and places her groin close to his eyes for him to see a man's testicles in his face.

"It takes two how we do it."

Ignacius jumps, he can see when a wig stands up on his oiled condom.

He takes a good close look at women in the room to be post-op transgender women.

When the bus driver goes through a pothole on the road side it makes it a soft shake for Ignacius to open his eyes and learn about his dream.

He can feel his eyelids are a little heavy and his mouth feels dry.

***

When Ignacius returns he tells others he has a need for fresh air.

"I am going out to a shop."

"You bring me some soda."

"Is there anything we need?"

Ignacius asks before he closes doors behind him.

He has no knowledge yet to understand their apartment is under surveillance of metropolitan police.

He walks across Husan gardens to a convenience store and when he steps to traffic lights on the sidewalk he is arrested.

The police car slides across the footpath giving a moment of sirens before he takes a look at them.

He is now resting face down on top of a police car when his hands are twisted backwards for handcuffs.

A day later he is thinking how are everyone doing and where are they?

He himself reached a softer sentence with his defense if he pleads guilty before the crimes and will be extradited.

But little did he know the reality he was facing and the faith awaiting him when he stepped into the courthouse.

Before he was able to learn where the shots got fired his head was covered in black linen back and he ran outside the court.

When his eyes catch a glimpse of sunshine in the courtyard he can see in his view a van with a logo written 'Tamagochi Tools'.

He can see now next to him Sakura standing and she is taking him inside their transport.

"It has been a long time no see."

Simon starts the engine and begins to drive away from their crime scene.

"That biatch Sakura with submachine Uzi walked to my court case. She shot the judge, prosecutor and my defense lawyer."

"I came to replace him. He was no good." Sakura is looking at him.

"Imagine your Korea."

Mage is cutting Ignacius' handcuffs off.

Ignacius laughing rubs his wrists.

"It is like a porn movie."

"How about some soju?"

Mage passes couples bottles around from the box back to his teammates.

When they noticed police activity they relocated further downtown in the outskirts of Seoul.

The orchid was near and they kept Sin On's body.

***

Within the attempt to create conviction for one of our heroes the time passed for the deadline and the unexpected incident had changed the path of their course.

Simon and Mage went desperately for clues to make one last attempt before the nuclear winter unfolds over the ground they are standing on.

But they only did have their last drinks at the pool party from a couple local bars they did visit when Mage mobile in secure line on the phone did ring.

"Hello."

"This is NATO Vice-Commander Mark, do you copy Live Wire?"

"Copy that Commander."

I have VIP on another line, and listen carefully to the information."

"Live Wire it is Kim Boom Boom."

"Copy that."

"I understand you are on an important mission therefore we assign flexible time and date to complete the rescue operation."

But in the background the party did not stop and girls were shouting at the end of the world party Boom Boom, let's have more drinks, Inquiry and Bad Bull.

They were referring to Mage and Simon, partially repeating what they did hear over the phone.

But Kim cleared his throat and did repeat his planned instructions.

"I understand your important job and we must receive the VIP package but time due is still limited nor plans are completely suspended and we would prefer to have the operation done."

"We understand and we are grateful for your clear instructions."

Once the phone call ended Ignacius and Sakura walked in through back doors of the garden to their pool party.

"We did worry so much about you guys and all we can find you guys surrounded by hot babes drinking to your death?"

"How did you find us?"

"We had a red line signal and GPS pointed us to your location to find HQ instructions for further instructions."

"Ahhh I see."

"Yayaya but what will happen now we are over the deadline."

Simon interrupts his worries.

"You can grab another bottle of soju and better sober up in the morning because we have got no much time to crack this case."

"Ignacius hey lovely ladies better pass me two because I am dry like sand for the last 12 hours."

Sakura sits down and observes the atmosphere before she drives them back early to avoid another incident with the local police department.

Ignacius is laughing and he is still drinking in the car on the way back to their hideout.

"yayayayayaya."

***

"Karateka karatedo."

"What do you mean senpai?"

"We will need to close in for failed attempted assassination of their ring leader Aisel Hasel Goon."

"How?"

"We give him a double barrel kiss on his shoulder then we run in Kansai style."

Two Walnut Generals

The rogue BBD Brit agent was having his dinner with his family after he made his last murder for retirement money from his field work.

He returned home to his loving family.

He was sitting in his apartment after dinner near TV drinking his glass of wine reading a book when his doorbell rang.

His wife opened the door and she asked for him because the delivery man said it was a special delivery for Edward Hogson.

He placed his wine on table and walked to the doorway for Ignacius let a straight shot off his suspender he was holding under delivery notice.

The clean shot left Mr Hogson skull and cut his wife's jaw off Ignacius stepped over letting her bleed to death on her wound.

He steps on the baby's neck while dying wife is holding in her arms. "I am sorry buddy, I let you go. You cannot live like this growing up alone like nobody."

***

A Metropolitan Police vehicle was parked inside a petrol station to pour petrol in their tank when one guy walked up to them asking in poor Hangul for directions to Central Locum Park.

He was holding a canister of petrol.

Police Officer attempted to guide the tourist but got hit in the back of his neck with a sack of rocks in black bag.

The Metropolitan officer thought his car broke and he needed assistance.

When his colleague steps outside to learn his partner is taking a short nap. His eyes turn black.

They drove with sirens on to their location holding a canister of petrol in their hands.

When they reached the location they turned off the sirens.

"It was a long time ago that I had a well run service vehicle."

"Let's light that prick on fire."

Ignacius steps out and makes a short run in the park.

Simon drives a round turning vehicle before he parks. He hears kicking and moving in the back of his trunk.

"You guys stop there. You will be living legends soon."

Ignacius runs past Sakura and blinks his eye leaving a petrol bomb on a bench near her.

She picks it up moments later and lights it on fire, throwing it under the feet of Aisel Hasel Goon.

The petrol bottle breaks under him and his security feet while they are running along the park.

"It is bento botelo for you."

Ignacius can hear a large explosion behind him and when he boards a police vehicle he laughs.

"I hope they brought their dancing shoes. These babies are on fire."

They let sirens on and blue lights flashing made a stop to pick Sakura up.

"Don't worry darling, there is no fuss from us."

Simon says when Sakura closes her doors behind her they drive off.

It takes not long for local police to learn about their missing vehicle for them to locate it for hot pursuit later in the evening.

While on RoofTop bar two men are having their drinks and are watching the landscape scenery below them.

"Brother Jack. I have not seen police transport performing Kansai Dorifto in a while."

"Yes, Ramolskis."

***

When they reached a breaking point at the end of their road they made a quick round turn, turning their long lights on.

They did gather a long police convoy after them near the end of the road.

When police transport got blinded by the light, it drove off in a chain reaction off the cliff.

"The cars off the cliff reminds me of WW2 SS style paramilitary march here like a trail of ants in Poland."

"Yes, the polished 'baklazani' to the waste container."

"Kawaii Senpai."

They hear Captain Mage reporting over the radio he can see them on a drone.

"It must be like bidding on pachinkos. You can never win."

Simon replies to his radio signal.

"Roger that."

***

They later established a connection with human slavery trafficers to their target.

It was the European War Criminal Polov Dune.

He is a thick businessman who specializes in trading illegal organs and sex workers he traffic to Eastern Europe.

His main objective was to establish crime links between Eastern Europe and the Korean Peninsula.

His shipping company in Poland was a great opportunity to establish a paper company in Southern Korea. He could build links with local outlaws.

He felt a great need to expand his crime syndicate; Mage finished his morning briefing of his unit.

"We show you war criminals."

"Let's give him death metal, Torpedo." Ignacius smiles looking at Simon.

"Choto Simon Senpai. Let's hear Mage Sensei's plan."

"I think we round them up and show them real war criminals like our Torpedo suggested."

"How do we do it? You always blame me on Live Wire."

"We will break Geneva's Convention of No War Weapons on the streets. They never will see it coming when the military hits them."

"What war weapons?"

"Team, you are familiar with how to pilot and execute army drones. I will provide additional training on how to print special assault rifles and make liquid bullets of high velocity and calibre."

"It sounds better by the minute."

"Ya Ya we can melt them to candle Wax once we need to dispose of them and print it again when we want it." Simon interrupts Ignacius.

"Once we confirm the rescue point. We start operating theatres shooting these actors' red foxes in red boxes."

"Roger that sensei we use codename to start operating under a red fox shooting these actors in a red box?"

"Yes I will update further because no plans survive in heat, only planning does."

The Discotheque

"We need to raid Aisel Hasel Goon nightlife spots."

"I delegate this task to Lord Ignacius and for rest we must follow the lead on Busan Courthouse case files."

"How about Eastern European war criminal Polov Dune?"

"I think he lost his religion. We clear his rat den once it comes to it."

When his team left for the Southern shores of the Korean Peninsula our Lord Ignacius set his planning in motion. He planned to complete his task for the morning briefing.

He chose a warehouse type venue in an abandoned industrial neighborhood to extract information the Live Wire team were investigating. With many houses made of caravan parks because of redevelopment planning it was a remote destination for cheap underworld entertainment park.

Ignacius made his way to start his dance under the disco ball. He said to himself.

"Good God gave me everything I want now I give everything to you."

He was looking to murder Eastern European War Criminal, Polov Dune.

The area was known for high crime rate and narcotics trade but his unknown attraction theme was tourists visiting his Discotheque.

Polov Dune was contemplating human trafficking within venue because it was his perfect hub to set traps to poor and vurnable he could pray on.

Ignacius passed the entrance pass to a Romanian drinking outside. He was able to see a woman sharing two men around the corner.

"A gypsies theme park? I am ashamed to know I am European. I have my resolve right now. I need to fix it."

The gypsies community was a perfect cover for Polov Dune to plan his crime syndicate works and station his work in Korea, he could obtain further market value.

Ignacius takes one step in his black suit wearing white collar shirt with the collar wide open and he is standing under a disco ball beneath the glass floor.

He is holding his grip for a colt handgun.

"Good God gave me everything I can give back to you." He shouts before he opens a calculated gunfire.

Outside travellers drunk community emotions were running high. They felt they must dispute their questions in fist fight.

One girl shouted for them to start and surrounded in the truck bay they began to fight.

"Start!" She shouted jumping up, raising her hand signal to start a street fight.

She was a Romanian woman who had a great passionate moment around the corner while Ignacius was entering the venue.

When everyone was running outside from gunfire to save their lives they were attacked by a drunk gypsies community because they thought they were being attacked by night goers.

They started swaying cars side to side.

Ignacius made his way to the top floor killing a couple security guards on his way up the stairways.

He learned paperwork they were seeking about human traffickers accounts and shipment dates were hidden in prestigious central Seoul offices. He held his documents.

He fired the final shot to accountants face before he left to report the situation in a phone call to Captain Mage.

The whole chaos of mass street fight breaking everything apart and setting their own caravans park on fire was devastating look to Ignacius eyes.

"Good God. They now set their own homes on fire after sharing their own family around these corners?" He spit on floor and left home before he was able to see more of carnage taking place after his mission.

***

It was an international case management document revealing their objective from the north was held in Busan pre-court detention center for trial for minor offences. The file Ignacius scouted over an internal network they found in public office papers in the Circulative Archives Department captured their attention.

It was not known to our four heroes that it was a trap Asel Hasel Goon had set up for them with Water Sots.

It was believed in Goon's information they were attempting to rescue a local drug baron with connections to the north to deal further damage to his cartel foundation.

Mage and his team felt for the diversion and were making an action plan to advance fast operation with set points to be completed before they will be able to return the hostage back to the north side of the Korean Peninsula.

It was early morning for Simon driving along Busan coast listening to local radio as he believed it was a local reporter briefing about a court case in Busan Courthouse.

"I am well on Live Wire."

"How are Wildflower and Torpedo?"

"I am set in location."

"The coast is clear and we should hit the target on set point."

The crowd outside the house of law was overcrowded with reporters and a police escorted armored vehicle was shielded with police protection to avoid hostility before retrial of the northern drug baron was complete.

Several death threats were reported when he was held in prison and local law enforcement took no chances neither to have him harmed nor seek aid for his escape.

But when they started walking away from the armored truck, police kept the line shielded away from cameras and curious passersby to the stairs in Busan's Court.

The 20 tons garbage truck with front fork lift drove in through closed off gates straight through the carpark crashing across prison armored transport driving further before it started making a turn.

The sudden panic started making a scene and police officers took hold of the inmate to carry him in before the unknown assailant turned around.

They made a run holding him on his feet and arms apart luckily enough to avoid escaping garbage truck plowing through tilted prison transport further pushing it out the way causing a scene of fear and confusion.

The full gear officers took in our inmate without waiting for him to stand up and they continued rushing him to the holding cell.

"It was a lucky escape or we would have had further casualties today."

Their radio was cracking with messages asking for reinforcements and briefing further about the situation.

The court alarm siren was on and court officers were asking journalists to walk inside the court building.

When they reached the holding cell and the officer was looking for keys to handcuffs and to cell doors, the inmate suddenly started to panic and was expressing heavy stress.

He was resisting to comply with an officer's attempt to calm him down, and he was making desperate attempts to bite and kick until blade pierces under helmet and out, dropping the officer to the floor.

Another officer was stabbed in the back of his neck kneeling before a lifeless officer's body to watch a silent drug baron holding on to his mouth with his eyes wide open.

Sakura did not waste much time to spray a drug across the drug baron's face within three seconds of him losing his consciousness.

Simon once finished checking officers pulse he stepped back to their objective to aid Sakura in escorting him out the building.

"Wait! I have their keys to the cell and his cuffs. We must throw those two officers in his holding cell to find more time until they notice in this chaos one is missing."

Simon passes the keys to the doors when he takes off the cuffs and covers his shoulders with a police jacket.

They continue rushing out asking to make way for an injured court officer escorting him to an ambulance waiting outside the building where Mage parked five minutes before garbage truck drove into the scene.

Mage is waiting outside ambulances van door's in first aid uniform waving them in when vehicle's sirens are on.

"Quicker guys, I want a drink out of this hell."

He sets keys in the ignition and starts driving away with Sakura and Ignacius checking vitals of the hostage they are attending in the patient's trolley.

But they came to realize in a hurry that the man they just took out of jail was too old to be the kid from the north their objective was set.

When the garbage truck plows them off the road, twisting the ambulance over three times, it mixes inside the emergency vehicle filled with shattered glass and medical equipment.

Mage was still holding heavy on his wheel watching his world turning upside down three times for him harder to see forward and feeling the blood dripping from his chin.

Slots jumped outside his garbage truck with two other men holding body bags to conceal the bodies they were about to take back in their truck cabin.

Sakura was attempting to stand up barely regaining consciousness pushing her arms up under a trapped trolley watching Simon's hands tangled in debris of shelves and his chest heavily pulsing.

Their passenger they took in rescue operation had fallen outside out the back doors and was not making any vital signs of life.

They boot kick her face to lose her vision.

A Grey Busan truck was parked across the road when Slots was closing the last body bag and was pointing to his assistant to reverse the truck.

Bibi Bit turned around when he was unable to receive any transmission from our Mage, and was able to see smoke coming out below the hill.

He turned gear in fourth transmission with a heavy feeling in his heart it was not right and a road accident did appear to falter their mission.

Third, turning off the hilltop he understood it was another garbage truck who just drove in his Litland Group attempting to escape and they are about to have them taken in for hostages.

His foot pressing deeper in the gas pedal he smashed out his way in the middle of the road parked truck turning his wheels sides. His foot gently holding the brake pedal twisted his truck backwards causing mountains of dust spraying over the road side.

He stepped out his truck and pulled out a telescope behind his belt in one swing extending it as he walked towards them.

The guy rushed towards the missed jab to Bibi Bit's face, getting his guts hit so hard he thought his inside was turned to a mash.

When Bit straightened his shoulder stance below he continued walking further to face Slots clenching his fists and with his finger gesture inviting a step closer.

Bibi Bit waved first false attempt to sway his combat stick, confusing Water Slots he missed and letting his guard have a bone breaking smash in his face shattering his jaw and eye socket along his jawline to his ear.

Bit stepped on his face with a light kick asking him who sent those fools to cause the incident.

"You are a dead man."

"I can see we are talking in a common tongue. Let's have a drink in a more comfortable place to tongue crap down further?"

He carries his gang of their bodies' bags in his garbage truck and straps Slots back in his body bag for further investigation.

It came time for our Mage to open his eyes to see Slots chained in chair sitting opposite the basement.

"Who could believe our countryman would pay us a visit? I am sure nobody would miss him. Ten times in a row changed identity with his criminal career, started robbing banks and now is a contract killer."

Simon walks closer to him with an 8 inch blade brushing the blank end along the captives face. He would prefer not to have hold of him because he was a high caliber killer chained in his basement but he knew from his active duty in the police force it was one in a lifetime opportunity to learn about him.

He takes off his tape on his lips and swings in the face handlebar of his blade removing two teeth splattering thick blood off his lips.

"Maybe you would be so kind enough to start a conversation with us, mister wanted criminal?"

"Who is talking? I am sure you are now most wanted in Korea."

"I am sure our Littland Jon Gi Sigis has far greater plans for you than us. Ya."

"Who the fock is this Jon Gi Sigis?"

Simon kicks ribs letting gasps of air from Slots lungs and explains to him Jon Gi Sigis is his uncle continuing interrogation further learning about the villain in his eyes.

"I cannot take people like you who make their living from killing for any price tag you Booble in internet. I would prefer to have your throat open now but we are waiting for our Jon Gi Sigis decision."

He pulls him across corridor in a cleaning locker room and turns lights off behind him closing the doors.

When his teammates feel awake enough to sit together and have further discussion about the epic failure of Aisel Hasel Goon's plan and their foolishness in the assault mission, they come to a conclusion.

They will operate War Theater, setting Aisel Hasel Goon their main objective because they will be wasting time if they seek any other outcome.

A while later in Holiday Jeju Resort SPA southern coast facility for VIP visitors on a sightseeing hill was parked Tamagochi Tools service van.

"Das it kontrollier."

"Copy you Torpedo."

"The streets are entering the SPA building."

"The streets do copy."

"Ya."

"Ahh."

The time a man was swimming breast strokes indoors pool but did he know our heroes were watching him.

He was exhausted from a recent case load in the National Prosecutors Office and decided to take time off in his favorite resort. When his mobile receives a call.

"Yes. I am off the case. You can call me in a week's time when I am back in the office."

"No. I am not available for disclosure to conclude the argument."

He hangs up and walks in the sauna room then takes a hot shower thinking he could use a steam room tomorrow.

He was standing in a changing room after a hot shower rubbing his hair off with a towel.

"Son will you pass me another clean towel from a rack behind you."

"You are a little young for exclusive members resort?"

"I am not your son, dear grandpa."

Ignacius is gently drawing out his round shaped blade from his neck whipping off the towel he offered him.

He took a towel and concealed his weapon to stab him through his throat and artery wounding him fatally.

He drops a blood covered towel over his face and takes him in a shower cabin letting stream of water on closing the doors behind him.

Ignacius changes to his gym clothes from swimming trunks and walking out the main entrance makes a phone call.

"Done done."

"Roger that the streets."

When all was done and said our four heroes were sketched and posted in the most wanted list.

The news was raising inland security concerns for four missing suspects to the highest police alert.

The time was when our Mage was browsing an internal information site seeing him lookalike and his teammates circulating the web he called his friends.

"Guys, I think we have our sketches."

Simon walks up to see his bald head and ruthless eyebrows sketched in lookalike manner, making him rub his bald head.

"I cannot believe I would turn into a celebrity overnight."

"Well what they say from pain to stars."

When Mage makes the comment he walks away planning to meet Ignacius in the meeting point and continue planning the route to find their Aisel Hasel Goon.

Simon follows behind him and makes a comment to adjust their war council planning.

"We should never again break our diamond formation in our unit!"

"Roger that."

***

But the day before they had a false lead in Jeju resort, Water Slots was meeting Aisel Hasel Goon and his prosecutor.

"I think Polov Dune would join us?"

"You know Polish Aubergine?"

Water Slots sits down and starts laughing.

"You have an interesting man of law on your side. He called my boss, therefore I came instead to resolve your problems for you because it was long before I had a great day relaxing in a spa."

A Romanian Theme Park

Simon closes his doors behind him leaving Water Slots injured in his chair. "I'll show you a good time later."

He brushes blood off his knuckles with a handkerchief and he sits on a stool outside taking his turn to take watch while his team is waiting for planning from NATO Vice-General Mark Ta.

"I hate not repaying my debts." He speaks under his breath.

When Sakura approached him, it was long in their operation; they had a bath.

She was intending to ask him where she could find a bathroom in the narrow underground basement facilities they were taking cover in an industrial site.

"Konnichiwa Simon Senpai. Have you been to Japan?"

"Ya."

"How was it?"

"We just sit in a club watching women working with hydraulics."

"What?"

"It was great."

"You just do not mind him." Ignacius walks near them and ear drops in conversation.

"I was thinking to ask you, how we wash because it was many days we were operating our field mission and we are managing a rescue operation."

"We have no showers here. It is only a former frozen meat hall. They kept a butcher's container and bathroom but because the site is an abandoned building. We have no commodities available."

"You take our wheels and have permission to visit Korean Spa." Simon hands her the keys from Tamagochi Tools.

They painted over in black and exchanged license plates.

She walks away and Ignacius sights looking at her. He thinks about her in the Hansun Apartments where they stayed together.

He captures their moments together; they lived in comfort.

"I have a bad feeling about this one."

Why?"

"Simon we are in wanted fugitives list and she is taking a Spa?"

"Who cares? She is a big girl."

He walks away and continues dreaming about her. He thinks about her memories and thinks about how he was looking at her.

***

She drives in Tamagochi Tools further off industrial neighborhood to Korean Baths Spa.

She walks in and handles her request for a hot bath.

Sakura Uto walks into the dressing room and takes off her blue jeans and blue shirt. She folds them together.

She loosens up her black satin bra and slides her underwear off. Sakura folds them and has a shower brushing her arms round her neck feeling fatigue from the last few days.

She rubs under her arms and her breasts thinking how long they will carry on for the lost Korean hostage.

"Yamite problem you." She thinks to herself and once wraps herself in white towel she walks wooden floor feeling her feet are tiny compared to Simon Senpai.

The doors open and she walks past a couple Korean girls in the sauna room. They were smiling and talking to each other.

She sits on sauna second layer floor attempting to steam off her pressure. "I wonder how long before Mage Sensei will finish coordinate our assault plan." She thinks about Lord Ignacius. He would be lookalike without his beard with our Captain Mage.

Sakura Uto rubs her shoulders and feels resting her arms on her legs wearing white towel only before she closes her eyes resting her head and shoulders on her neck to hot sauna walls.

"It is great in sento."

Lord Ignacius' imagination about her in the Hansun Apartment wearing glamorous but simple clothes and her minimal interaction made her mysterious; he refused to think about her.

He actually remembered his dream in the local bus from the action point he took on the way back.

"I would love her wide open pumping in back of Tamagochi Tools before we go out to wash in sauna to recharge our batteries to do it again in back."

She did rescue him from a courthouse but he did not say thank you and decided to have her after sauna take her for a glass of Soju.

He was wondering what her underwear looked like, how short she was. How her chest unfolds she takes her top.

He was willing to have sex with her because she felt different not like a woman he cut throat in Osaka love hotel.

"She was a biatch. She brought a blade to her first date." Lord Ignacius felt discussed and spat on the floor taking his watch on a stool near the door where they kept Water Slots.

"I wonder how long before Jon Gi Sigis will order Pioter or Vlad to toss your corpse out!" Ignacius becomes aggressive and slaps his fist at the door behind him; they kept their war prisoner.

He continues to shout. "Our Littland Group is no joke, you motherfocker."

"What? Do you have something to say? You want me to fock your mother? I will make sure she kisses you on the lips after!"

A few moments later Mage walks in and fires a fatal shot in Water Slots forehead.

He walks out past Lord Ignacius not looking at him.

"Why did you kill him so quickly?"

"One point was you guys were loud enough to wake me up; and second I realized we have no use for him."

Simon walks in drinking his cup of coffee looking at both of them. "I came here to relieve you on watch but I can see your future now."

Mage walks away while Simon Says interrupts their conversation.

"What future?"

"You and Sakura Uto are going on a hot date tonight to toss this corpse away before tomorrow."

"I am not in threesome necrophilia."

"I know you don't, but tomorrow we riot. You better fock her good tonight in our Tamagochi Tool."

"Do not forget to warm her up in a tent with Soju before you get lucky around the corner heading back." Mage walks by looking at the logistics of tomorrow's operation.

Ignacius smiles and brushes his fingertips over his large beard.

***

They planned erupt chaos in a midst of disarray murder Aisel Hasel Goon because he was a stepping stone to free their hostage.

"Aisel Hasel Goon should rot in prison before his last minute to the gallows."

"I think we take care of him in a military style."

"Roger that Torpedo. How are you approaching Streets?"

"I am closing in, Live Wire."

Daily Bong News wrote past few days near their abandoned industrial site hideout were held a joint protest attempting bring awareness to fault play in construction safety laws honesty in workplace and demonstrate opposition to demolish further neighborhoods apart industrial sites to prevent local unable afford housing once evicted.

Lord Ignacius places his white safety helmet on and wears a facemask.

Meanwhile Aisel Hasel Goon planned to oversee local mercenaries and disband the protestors so they could begin demolishing buildings.

He drives in the next lane and tilts his garbage truck Bibi Bit had repaired since the Busan incident.

Lord Ignacius smashes his wheels hard and drives over Aisel Goon escort car side crushing partially top and sides ripping to parts.

He continues to drive past Aisel Hasel Goon eviction team and in he hits redevelopment team planning booth before he stops.

Aisel Hasel before Ignacius crashed in his convoy was stepping out his car to oversee eviction done before day ends he could complete a contract to start building a business.

Simon on the side of the building wearing a protesters vest throws a petrol bomb.

He set on fire construction trucks blocking exits and causing further flames creating conflagration engulfing eviction workers jackets and shoes.

They charged protesters before more petrol bombs lit on, holding wooden beams hitting the first protester over his jaw, making two groups start a street fight.

"I think we have riots."

"Copy that. I spotted an enemy."

"Go go go… You take the point."

Sakura Uto in police uniform stabs to death Aisel Hasel Goon.

She walks closer to him. Metropolitan local response units made their way and she hid amidst them in their shadow, not taking her eyes off her prey.

Aisel Goon was surrounded with his security escorts holding them aside to an undamaged vehicle planning their escape once police cleared route from flames and debris of fighters grabbing and holding on each other throwing their fists and sticks.

"You clear those fools! How they can do this. I'll make them pay!"

Aisel Goon felt a short prick on his side from a policewoman wearing a face mask attempting to assist to clear an area from violent protesters reported causing riots.

"I think she stabbed him."

"Roger that."

"Wildflower stay in your position."

"We make a point."

The voices were spilling over a secure earpiece radio channel.

Aisel Hasel felt a sharp cold breath filling up his lungs. He felt he was breathing out ice from the side of his lungs to his brains.

He felt to floor his security holding on him attending and aiding him see him convulsing on soil letting white foam out his mouth. They were watching his white eye balls.

The Tamagochi Tools transport drove off the side of the broken building. It was hidden behind cartoon waste camouflaging a partially open part of an industrial site.

He drove pass near and stopped for one protester open door and wait for others to board Tamagochi Tools vehicle.

Lord Ignacius ran to Sakura Uto wearing a construction helmet and mask.

He wielded a 20 inch plumbers tool opening back of remaining Aisel Hasel Goon assistants skulls breaking other faces to make a way for Sakura Uto escape with him.

Ippon

Within Western Seoul a telephone booth had several calls when a call was made to an empty booth.

A curious passerby answered an unknown caller and made the surrounding area filled with smoke and emergency sirens.

Simon a few hours before his team planning completed preparations for black operation Black Dunes completes his last packet of smoke.

He parked their tools van in a small residential street around the corner from a busy road.

He took his bomber jacket wearing black face mask and hat to his location and placed explosives in a telephone handset in a corner booth not well visible but in use.

"I am going to fix this booth with a bomb in a handset. It should make them wake up before we hit the account hole."

"Roger that. You make sure it does not go off before you place it in offline mode."

"Ok."

He hangs up a secure line call from his captain and walks in a booth, takes the call handset off and tapes it temporarily black call button on.

He opens the handset microphone part and replaces it with a similar but smaller wired version adding extra to microphone wire C4 explosives.

He high wires it back by cutting old cables off and twisting them with bomb wires.

Simon screws handset microphone part back on and gently lifts black wire off to make sure there is no surge to activate C4 he swapped with the original microphone.

"It should add good gunpowder."

Their intentions were to blow up explosives gathering major attention to the other side of Capital before they will make an appearance in the commercial part of Capital attempting to uncover Eastern European war criminal Polov Dunes money laundering office to find transaction details they could trace hostage tracks.

He walks back in their van round the corner and gets inside.

"Are you sure it will work and nobody will decide to use it now?"

"I watched it for two days on a local store CCTV we broke in online."

"I hope we should be fine or we just end up causing mayhem in Korean Madness before we find a lost kid and make our debut in our first track and trace rescue field."

"Yes. It is our first operation together."

Simon Says tapes Daily Bong News newspapers over his waist, lays in a double layer over his bottom leaving a triple layer on his crotch. He then pulls up his pants.

Ignacius continues looking at him thinking a little did he knew since their childhood friendship.

"You can never be ready enough for those motherfockers."

.

"Hello my name is Gorimo Lopez."

They walk in a planned meeting in financial street to see account services.

They take a seat and Lord Ignacius asks if he could make a call because he forgot his mobile phone back in their car.

He takes a couple minutes before the connection dials a call handler and the signal shuts off on the other side of the line.

"a?"

He places the office phone down and walks back to the waiting room.

Simon walks out their waiting room a moments later to kick on the floor one accountant.

He continues kicking his face open with his black polish shoes to wipe blood off.

He places his arms back in his suit pockets and asks where Polov Dune is hiding the slush funds in the accountancy office.

"Where is the polished possy now?"

Accountant bleeding on the floor covering his face, looking away trembling in fear not to meet Simon's gaze.

His blood running out his nose and with a broken nose he cannot see it clearly feeling the adrenaline rush he attempts to answer.

"I am sorry I do not understand?"

"I will ask you one more time!"

Ignacius walks out behind the waiting room glass door and opens his assault rifle fire in the office sealing before the office manager manages to answer Simon's query.

"Where are polish barbies!"

He screams once he shoots an open round of fire and points his high velocity caliber automatic weapon to workers standing up behind their desks.

.

The literature agents arrived in black European class limousine. They were wearing black suits.

One opened an assault rifle fire on the street to collect data from next door war criminal Polov

Dunes slush fund accountancy office next door to the literature house.

But before then they walked into our office.

They felt a warm couple of businessmen including their translator who stood by their side.

She was Asian, of Japanese descent. She was polite and curious and led them to our office facility on the top floor.

One asked us to use our office telephone because he forgot his mobile phone back in their business car.

He said it was an important call. He was about to make an important business transaction before we had aggression broken out in our workplace.

His colleague walked out and broke my nose talking and asking questions without making any sense of reality.

He walks out a moment later filling our office full of gun shells pointing his weapon at us.

"I believe he introduced himself a Gorimo Lopez. I am not sure. I must check our guest list for visitors."

"We make them Black Friday sale they will never forget." He spoke before I escorted us to our office floor pass literature house.

I think they were literature agents or creative writers who approached our services because they needed our accountants' help.

They spoke very creatively, their prose was original voicing ideas across making vocal points like an artist's.

"Let's give them some metal."

"Ahh ya."

"We have plenty of change, ya."

I truly believed they were planning something big like a good rock concert.

"It will be ok for now and stay in the ambulance to make sure paramedics check your nose. It looks like a real bad injury."

"Thank you officer."

.

Lord Ignacius opens a live fire on the street. They just left the office building block in a hurry.

He shot a ginger woman while making their way on the street.

The time crime reports came in about calls of crimes within a very same time committed in different parts of Korean Capital.

"White collar crime division one."

"We have heavy fire on the streets from literature agents outside publishing house."

"Do they cook books?"

"No."

"Wrong department."

Ignacius pierces a clean shot dead on the street in ginger woman.

Simon walks to a metropolitan police officer behind him on the sidewalk who is planning to aim his firearm at Lord Ignacius.

"You think a stab vest will save you from me cutting a peninsula out from your legs. You should have thought better, my friend."

He cuts in and lets out a sea of blood from hanging partially erupted testicles. Simon smiles and walks away.

Their escort transport is parked around the corner and the driver is waiting inside already with their translator.

"I wonder how they are doing there?"

He finished eating his sandwich.

"I think Simon went too far using high velocity explosives in a public place."

"A, I believe we broke a Geneva Convention of No War weapons in peaceful streets."

"Yes. He bombed a suicide telephone booth. You look! It looks like they are running to us."

Sakura Uto is able to see Lord Ignacius in black suit with Simon wearing a matching pair of black sunglasses running with black bags packed in their guns.

"How was it?"

"You press the gas pedal. I think Simon cut the officer's balls off while I kept shooting live rounds to make us look like we robbed them."

Captain Magnum Mage starts to drive, indicating he is turning his vehicle left; they continue to drive outside Southern Seoul to avoid traffic and take time to examine evidence.

"But how about the evidence we planned for?"

"I stole it off their barbie but first I had to twist and turn Ken's arms well."

"I think the explosives used by Senpai were a bit much for us to blow up the phone booth."

"Ahh you do not worry about it. I am lately acting crazy because of jetlag. I am in a Korean Madness mindset."

"It is a form of mind set?"

"Ya you do not worry about him. He can be like this."

"He told you our real names because he felt might not live much longer through our mission together."

Lord Ignacius places his hand over Sakura's shoulder in the front seat while Magnum Mage is driving their vehicle.

He thought to reassure her because everybody felt psychological strain left in harsh unknown conditions in the environment; only their Captain Magnum Mage felt familiar comfort.

Hold Your Beer Boys

"Let's open the next time a paranormal agency kakatwo."

"Ya Lord Ignacius it would be a great idea to take cover as paranormal psychos."

"Ah, I think our Captain Mage would be our sanitar."

Sakura Uto and Magnum Mage are looking at them while counting their bullets.

"Let's move out in five. We have to catch war criminal before his tracks gets cold and we end up nuclear waste."

They board Tamagochi Tools van painted in rainbow colours with sticker on side, Sex Tools from Tamagochi.

"Why are we sitting in pink seats and the front panel is pink?"

"Dear Captain Mage, we are under scrutiny of budget and we're not able pressed for time to steal a better van, we could mark our tools van."

"Simon drop your English. I know your englese is poor but mimic in pink driver's seat is awful."

They start four liters petrol engine pistons pumping sparks and letting black steam out their chimney they drive off in rainbow assault van.

A little later it felt too hot for them to experience a combat situation while Sakura Uto were attempting to decipher encrypted files in Polov Dune's office upstairs.

Our team were ambushed in Polov Dune's mansion corridor from both entry points of left and right.

Magnum and Lord are taking cover from heavy fire responding with SIG MG tactical team rifles.

When Simon kicks the vent in and throws explosives in.

"Here is a glory hole for you, dirty Poles."

"Kurva!" They shout. The security team is running and jumping for cover but little too late.

Lord Ignacius replies to their screams before the explosion sets motion in silence. "Take that kurva."

Simon Says sits on top of the mountain of bodies he pulled in one place from a high charged grenade explosion.

"I always wanted to smoke a cigarette on a pile of dead bodies." He ends his cigarette smoke in the dead man's eye.

"Where are your heads now, criminals?"

Simon looks at them, all dead, thorned to pieces left in one big piece of dead meat, with eyes looking for a scream of mercy looking at nothing but faint air.

"You know until they will not tell us where the hostage is, we kill them." Magnum Mage let's his arm on Simon's shoulder before he checks his wrist watch to see what is taking so long our Lord Ignacius drive the Tamagochi Sex Toys van up the front door.

"We are now war criminals hunters, sensei?"

Sakura Uto slowly walks from top stairs looking at Simon and Magnum Mage. She is wearing black Swiss tactical gear, black and in grey strips of camouflage.

"How was it?"

"I have our VIP ID location time and date, the coordinates they will move their convoy in longitude and latitude somewhere along the coast."

"I see, yes we are hunting monsters here."

"Let's lock and load." Simon places a new cartridge in and loads a new shell a seconds before Ignacius pulls over outside forest mountains remote mansion doors.

"You look hot." Lord Ignacius looks at Sakura Uto behind the pink wheel and smiles with his large beard.

^.^

"We need more muscle before we start our debut to take the kid back."

"I hope he will be happy back home in the north otherwise I end up going on a rampage over there after all those piles of bodies we left in the south to have peninsula saved."

"I think I know one candidate."

"What sensei?"

"We have a very great tour guide, you remember our Bibi Bit. He is half Korean and Thai."

"Ahh I see. He was a very great garbage truck driver."

"Maybe he knows more tour guides could aid sabotage their illegal human trafficking business before we kill them and rescue poor kid?" Lord Ignacius resumes the topic after Magnum Mage interrupted his conversation with Simon Says.

Simon pulls out a stolen mobile phone from one dead body left back in the mansion and dials Bibi Bit.

"Where did you get this phone?"

"I took it off the corpse and a couple piles of wons, these 500000 grannies are looking great."

"They must be old." Sakura Uto laughs, holding her breath in from Simon's poor joke.

"I was worried you lost your sense of judgement and spent your money on a phone they would track us."

They all start to laugh from Captain's Magnum Mage joke.

°.°

"I am very happy to introduce my cousin , Ugis Tako, he is a fisherman slash human smuggler."

They smile and greet him but he does not speak looking at them with a straight face.

"I forgot to say he does not speak English."

He smiles. Captain looks at him and guides them to the rainbow van they stole.

"Let's talk inside before we continue any form of business."

They meet in the mountain's peak forest car park inside a geographical forest site.

"I will need all your mobiles inside my bag we could start working in confidential details. Arigato."

They board their vehicle and Simon hands out piles of cash to both subcontractors to make instalment payment before they start working.

"You know we are a very confidential business known as Littland Group. Our Jon Gi Sigis is a very well connected business leader who is willing to appreciate your help."

^.^

Ignacius is walking through an alleyway and can see an old man sucking with his grey hair a black penis, half erected elder attempting to suck it up.

He sucks in from his nose a snot and spits on the floor.

"You are spitting in an image?"

"I never expected to see it."

"I hate killing time off work walking on old Seoul streets in party neighborhoods."

"I am not sure if we saw a party over there. It is a more raw horror we witnessed."

"Yes but we all can do is drink our beloved Soju and appreciate Korean barbecues before scheduled time of operation."

"Yes we cannot attract any attention before we finish our mission and take our leave back to the sunny shores of Thailand under palm trees."

"I hope Mark Ta will not draft too soon NATO SS Spartacus to pick us up."

"I am not worried about this right now but I am thinking if Police Dune was not clever enough to learn we are not after his money but cargo."

"I hope Ugis Tako is reliable enough as Bibi Bit describes."

"I miss Sakura Uto company. She said she must sleep extra longer before she recovers from combat stress fatigue."

"You look over there. I can see another great tent of Soju."

Simon shows the pouring sign with his hand at his mouth and both smiles rubbing their hands.

"You keep your mouth where your money is."

"I still have some left from those corpses."

They both burst into laughter.

When a radio signal comes through from Captain Mage.

Kenpai

"Kenpai." Simon Says drinks his cup of Soju.

"I wonder who is Ugis Tako."

"I am not sure but he looks no clown.'

"Yes he is not talk a lot type guy."

"Let's drink that and to our unit."

"Simon, you remember our school days and now we are sitting here enjoying our Soju."

"Yes, from tea bar to Osaka nightlife, Thailand palm trees to beer tents in Seoul."

"Yes a lot happened along the way but Magnum Mage never changed."

"Yes but he is now our Captain."

"Yes he has something in him."

"We met so many people in our lifetime thanks to him."

"Yes I can now carry a duty firearm once more."

"Yeh, one is illegal and only purpose to murder." Ignacius drinks his cup of Soju.

"To NATO units." Simon raises his hand to Soju.

Ignacius takes his drink and turns his gaze away one hand concealing his cup.

"Is it some sort of secret concealed drinking technique they taught you, I missed out on?"

"No, it is a local custom."

"Let's drink to that."

They both conceal their lips while looking away from each other drinking.

"Let's laugh until the day we die, because the moment of death defines how we lived our lives."

"Yeh Simon, it is great news we live a good life."

"Death is writing its own bestsellers. You are welcome to northern european mind games."

"Yes, let's drink to that."

"Yes. Cheers this beer tastes so great after uncountable bottles of Soju."

"Hey. Let's go Gamnden town. I hope Polov Dune gets down sooner."

"Let's take a shat outside his house."

"You are talking a bunch of shat I do not want to hear."

"How we deal with him."

"We just break his face."

"I heard about cultural masks."

"What about them? Are they the facemasks everybody wears so as not to cough on each other?"

"I place my hands up. I surrender. We poop in his mouth like a storm in the desert."

"Nice. Ignacius, you talk more now like a bent Lithuanian copper."

"Well I am not a copper hole."

"Are you talking about atomic number 29?"

"Let's drink more of that. I am happy tonight."

"The massacre and craze horror in Seoul got me tired. I am tired of this mission to attempt to discover the situation and provide safe extraction once the package is secure and heading home."

"You are talking now like a law professor Ignacius. Here is more Soju for you."

"The Communist government is planning a retaliation with missile launch and this can bring serious casualties. Therefore the elite squad was assembled for an important task. But we cannot understand how we can not do it?"

"Maybe we are not elite?"

"I drink for that."

"The new Latvian passports with fake identity and UN detective licenses issued for 3CIIA agency. Is a great cover but we need assistance and Mark Ta is a low profile when it comes to resources."

"Yes our Vice-General is a proper commando willing us watch to do the same."

"Mage is Algimant Bravo. You Vlad Tango. I am Pioter Romeo."

"You do not have to tell me your ridiculous name."

"Yes, our pseudonyms are horror storylines here."

"Yes and our fake Latvian passports looks like great copies."

"Here are resources gone." Ignacius closes his crotch after a couple shakes and taps Simon still standing behind the urinal lavatory. He reaches the faucet before walking, swinging back to his open bar stool have more Soju.

"We face the face of adversity from local corruption sustaining the prevention of truth."

Simon walks behind him. "We show them local corruption."

>.>

"If you trip over the rock do you blame the rock?"

"No?"

Captain Mage asked his unit in the morning.

"I need good help to save me from my headache once I drank so much last night."

"We are compromised. I think Polov Dune has a snitch in the NATO army. He learned about us and we are now heading to kill him before North drops us a nuke."

"Well at least he dies too then." Simon places his morning coffee on the table.

"The bully does not know what is to be punched unless you return the favour." Sakura Uto pours a cup of morning Expresso.

"I am confident he was unaware we are here on top of a confidential mission but I am confident he is thinking we are up to no good and off duty."

"Let's show him how we work in NATO."

"Ok. I start a silver fox hunt."

"Let's call Bibi Bit and Ugis Tako to start their bit on a mission."

=.=

Lord Ignacius breaks the bus driver's face in a steering wheel while on the road.

"It is only the beginning men."

Because they kidnapped him on the way to a shop.

"Those Polov Dune's men are pigs." He finishes smacking the local bus driver's face into the steering wheel from the smoking bus with the engine crashed in a tree. "How I will go out with Sakura with this broken nose."

He breaks polish man's neck before he leaves public transport.

"I went out on a date to meet Sakura. She could give me a lift with Tamagochi Tools."

But sadly our hero, Lord Ignacius, was targeted as a potential victim in Polov Dune's plan.

His counter strike team targeted him in the darkest hour sending his war criminals to follow him and let him board a fake bus to have him kidnapped and tortured to death before he let them know where others were hiding.

Ignacius walks in a bus and can see doors closing behind him to see men standing up wearing facemasks holding claw hammers pointing to him. "What?!"

Lord Ignacius shouts, he kicks the first killer in a bladder knocking him backwards to other assailants hands.

He grabs his claw hammer and murders them both opening and fracturing their skulls over 60 times.

He walks to another one both preparing to play their death dance of fatal hammer swings.

Him missing a shot at Ignacius forehead he goes under and twists his hammer to a claw side sliding his hammer in huge swing force through his neck jaw bone in.

Ignacius rips his neck open pulling open his neck kicking him down.

"You better get down."

He is looking in a passenger mirror and can see a bus driver watching him watching him.

He swings his hammer side arm twisting his waist sideways and hammers the driver's poor look on his face before the hammer reaches him.

"It is a proper ninja action." He whispered to himself, holding a slight smile on his lips.

The bus loses control without a conscious driver, swaying to the sides until it reaches the final destination in the sidewalk pine tree.

He stands and loosens his neck up and stiff shoulders. Ignacius can see two left remaining polish men bleeding out their bodies crushed in a debris of seats smashed together.

They are bleeding out their legs, shoulders and chests pierced through in a steel debris peeking out of debris of seats.

He checks his bleeding hand and can feel a stiff palm feeling unable to move one of his left fingers. He walks to the bus driver to pick his head up with his injured left arm.

"It is your lucky day that I am right handed." He continues to punch the driver's face until he starts to hit his head on a wheel.

"It was a proper collision." He jumps out the front broken window and makes a run for Tamagochi Tools transport.

^.^

When Sakura reaches a driveway in the planned meeting point, could Simon provide first medical aid because he was trained to nurse under active military heavy fire.

Simon opens his van doors and asks Ignacius to step out. He could show them first his new weapon they made to arrange to blow up the whole building with war criminals inside. They could finish their mission.

"It should help us finish our Korean Madness and get back home sooner in one piece."

Simon Says arranged water truck filled ballistic missiles.

"WTF!?"

"World Taekwondo Federation?"

"No. My arm still hurts like a biatch after polish criminals kidnapped a whole bus to kidnap me."

"No worries. We kill them quickly to conceal our identities. We have already arranged a transport for our 'hostage' back." Captain Mage walks out of the construction site booth wearing a helmet.

"Are we making a test shot?"

"No Ignacius, we would slam the whole district in dust. We keep it for better use to aim and fire like proper snipers.'

^.^

Our heroes are sitting in the background of whole madness attempting relax, tell stories and their dreams before their storyline continues to accomplish their fears.

"I have had no dreams for the last few weeks."

"No worries. I think under heavy active fire you lose the comfort of dreaming. You just sleep heavy."

"What made you choose NATO, Mage?"

"I guess to quit dreaming."

"Nice but how about other jobs like working in a kitchen like Ignacius."

"How about now you all ended up together working under me? I think I was made for this job."

"Yes I am sure when in life you worked in one job it feels like it was made in a laboratory bottle."

"You think it is to work in black operations? You just count your bullets and enjoy moments. You get to travel."

"I made a decision to bring Law and Order but now I have become a traveller."

"You do not worry Simon. I think under your request our Nato General made a scrutiny under close look and tracked those corrupt cops who made you guilty."

"Really?! What?! What happened to them next?"

"They are dead already because it was too difficult to find them guilty in the house of court."

"It serves them well. I knew I never took bribes."

"I know I am sure lies get to your reality."

"How about you Mage? You are always silent like a rich family butler. You never talk a lot, never show us much of what you think."

"We are here as a part as friends to get closer."

He stands up and walks away and takes another bottle of water. He looks around.

"Spring is coming and we have two days to finish. We will fall in the rainy season back in Thailand."

°.°

When Mage was holding a conversation with Simon Says, our Sakura Uto and Lord Ignacius were standing under an old industrial sign written in English, Advertising Rams.

"Is it a Black Jack card game illegal casino?"

"Yes I think we can gamble here for information and double our spending money."

"Yosh, let's go in baka."

"Great. Ignacius-san your Japanese is getting better."

"Bingo. We are just on another great date."

"Yamite, you make blush."

"I do not think it is kawaii to take you in gambling house on our third date after those War Criminals made me late to our second date."

"Yes."

"To keep in our mind the first date was to drop a dead polish killer's body. I think we are improving in our relationship."

"Yamite baka, like we are dating in a first place."

He smiles and taps her back.

"I know we are work colleagues but our professionalism should not get in our way."

"Let's gamble first, Ignacius."

"Ya, it is like Lithuanian parliamentarians talks full of steroids."

They walk in the building.

Internal Inferno

Simon Says is browsing his mobile device.

"Is there any info about our next move?"

"No, just Marquis Kebab the Lithuanian Foreign Minister up to no good...ah what a disgusting and nothing new."

"Simon, you should stop reading tabloids."

"Yes, Lord Ignacius, we should stop knowing about our Foreign Minister shatting all over the place."

"Whahaha, he is no good. I know about it."

"I think we should do him SAS style."

"No, it stinks too much."

"We then lick his possy."

"You said it brother. The first meal after a long way home."

.

Our Sakura Uto's heroes, the three samurais from White States, have fallen in danger once more. They need assistance.

"Kawaii my ronins."

"Ah ranin? Is it a bad joke in foreign language?"

Simon Says finish his can of black fizzy drink.

"Let's roll this dice and see fear in the enemy's eyes."

"Magnum Mage say something."

"It is magnetic when you talk about taking him in and slaughtering him."

"It would be Lord Ignacius' wedding pig."

"You guys must talk about Ignacius stag night too with Foreign Minister's family."

"Shhh...you keep quiet about it."

"Not kawaii at all."

Sakura laughs out loud

^.^

When Ramolskis and brother Jack reappear to save the day from evil polish.

"It's like the times we nailed the Tabor chief Large Dick and his mental brother to the first apartment door with his wooden leg."

"Nope it will be like we felt his wife in the back of our car seats."

"Yeah, we spread and butter her over there."

"She was such a lick I thought she had her jaws open all day all over my Dick. It felt like dying off."

"Yeah and I had to hold his two kids hands behind the corner until you finished in the freezing Klaipedos cold."

"Yeh Memel memo fun."

"I squeezed right hard in her avoiding your seamen on her lips. It took some time to drill open. I think he has cockles dick or something."

"Yeh, what a loser. I had to pound her for two hours until this fake blond felt enough."

"Yes, I took a snapshot of her red bottoms."

"Yeh, keep a picture, it will last longer than such whore."

"Hahaha, what a fun time. We should kick her longer, like a can down the road and visit her to pick these losers kids after school to give her lift back."

Ramolskis spat on the floor.

"It is like on her possy."

"Hahaha...you're right."

"Is this the best Klaipeda has yet?"

"I am not sure yet."

"I think he has a brother in prison, a proper prison rat."

"Yeh, I hope he has a good chick to share too. You know they turn lonely and their vacuum closes after a while."

"I would love it to slide open."

"Yes, brother Jack."

•.•

Simon let's pass his guard behind his back to see a hanging window shard to see him charge from behind.

He was holding his handgun under his armpit to blast opponents skull open in a blood splatter.

"I hate these voodoo dolls." Lord Ignacius shouts in his shorts outside their hotel window to Simon Says.

They shot a Polish war criminal attempting to assassinate them in an alleyway.

Simon was walking in the evening to bring a couple bottles of Soju back when he noticed a suspicious male in his forties following him.

In 166 street he took left to walk past their Tamagochi Tools to walk faster ahead of his drawing his handgun out.

He stabs him in the neck holding on his hand Simon slowly pushes a glass shard in his neck the whole of his body down lowering dying body to floor looking in his eyes to keep him silent.

He takes a look at the glass shard in cold body's neck six meters apart and can see another killer.

He lets his arm in armpit and fires a fatal shot.

"You look guys? Do I have only myself to clean up all this shat?"

They close their windows and do not respond.

"I was only willing to bring a few drinks now but I have to disinfect two bodies before this cheap hotel concierge comes back."

Ignacius shouts out his window. "You blame this Polov Dune!"

"I swear I cut his balls out."

"Can we bring back Bibi Bit?" Magnum Mage spoke outside his window with Simon.

Sakura Uto did not pay attention and continued to sleep under sounds of homicide.

"Why?" Simons shouts back.

"I think he will have his cousin Ugis Tako let Lord Ignacius have his wife while the Polish loser enjoys his bubble bath."

Lord Ignacius opens his window suddenly. "Really?"

"Yes and let's not shout in poor Seoul because we do not know how many Lithuanians can live here."

"Ya, let's head back to Bavaria once we finish our beer."

.

When our Simon is reading Daily Bong News and reading in between pages he bad mouth their trails of crime making them look stupid.

Lord Ignacius treats him to one punch he finally shuts up.

"I told you to keep your mouth shut."

"I know this duty stress gets to us all but next time choose your nickname to Smok Sensei."

He brushes his jaw after a straight punch and takes a drink from his water bottle and collapses to the floor.

"I think those Polish asshollleeeesss will pay."

Ignacius casts his bottle aside picking up Simon off the shopping mall floor.

"I hope you will not make me late for my date. I am so steamed up, I bought a XXL size packet of condoms."

"You live my life my son." Simon attempts to speak with him before he drifts asleep.

They place narcotics in some of teammates' items to subdue them.

When Mage clears the path of the smoking gun.

He walks straight behind them firing vital shots in the back of their heads wearing black bomber jacket, jeans, baseball hat and medical face mask.

He kills two killers from Poland sitting in an indoor mall near them walking by their coffee table when he points his barrel to the third.

He presses it on his eye forcing him to press head on the table and fires a shot.

"This is what I call the demonic eye." Lord Ignacius looking stunned at Magnum Mage grabs Simon Says and makes his run.

^.^

Ugis Tako opens the hotel room 218 door and walks in, placing his service keys in his black suit pocket.

"Boss, are you there?"

Ignacius is checking his hair style and checked shirt open collar to stay neat in the elevator mirror taking it up to the second floor in the hotel facility.

Karateka

"Let's take Polov Dune's biatch south." Ignacius grooms his large beard in the mirror.

The war criminal's bodyguard enters his deluxe hotel penthouse suite.

"I think everything is ready for tonight's concert of native Korean theater. Your wife is getting ready next door Sir Polov Dune."

"You are a good boy. You have a good rest and smoke a cigarette. I will take a bath before I see my wife."

Ugis Tako closes his doors behind him and walks near the fire exit to have his smoke.

Ugis Tako infiltrates his crime office to be his bodyguard.

He can see Lord Ignacius pass near him. "We are taking the action card of aces. I am over and out."

Lord Ignacius nods his head seeing Mr Tako watch him passing by and smiles.

"I hope it will be 30 minutes ok?"

"I think it will be ok to see her like a prostitute."

"You do it in 15 minutes because she is hot."

"I have enough spandex gear, you do not worry about me."

He knocks on her doors and tells her he is her new special bodyguard. He enters and unzips his black jeans letting her know his mission.

"You do not worry sweetheart. I am your husband's special guest. He is very busy in his bathtub. I help you get dressed before you both sit holding hands watching a show."

"It is about time. He was so busy with his office work. I thought it would never happen."

Ugis breaks his bathroom doors in a hotel room and drowns him he could call medics to confirm his suicide death.

Mr Tako grabs a fire extinguisher near him once he finishes his smoke and runs inside the penthouse suite.

He breaks the bathroom lock and before he does it he wears his spandex gloves.

He places his face under water forcing him to fight to the death he cannot force his hands.

He is watching his expensive watch for how long he was under the water.

"I think our sweetheart is hot now. I think I have him swimming."

"You let Lord Ignacius finish and call medics once he leaves the love nest when he completes his mission. We want his death confirmed of suicide."

"Roger that. He is dead already. I cannot see his pulse. I had sleeping pills in his water. I ran in to see he took too long to see his wife. He was dead once I broke the doors open."

"Yes you do that."

"Thanks cousin. I shut the transmission now."

Bibi Bit was happy. His cousin made enough money they could never earn in one year working in tour guides.

Lord Ignacius next door is having an affair with his wife so she could keep shut her hole and make her pregnant.

"I wonder if Lord Ignacius will wear protection? You know he is hot blood."

"Let him have his fun. He had no luck with our Sakura."

"How is my Samurai Ignacius doing?"

"I think he is a great distraction."

"We should leave soon once he leaves the building." The Tamagochi Tools van was parked near Royal Plaza Holidays Resort In.

"I wonder how long he will take in her travelers in tavern?"

"I think war criminals' first wife is hot."

She was wearing white suit and black her he spread her tight office skirt apart. He took it out and stroked it.

He took no time slipping it in her legs apart tilting her long black hair to the side, how he slid her black undergarment to the side.

He felt her love skin slip in her forcing him to feel it tighter like never before.

"She really was not lying about this war pig." He thought to himself.

She was wrapping her legs tilting her hips in lock up forcing her spine to fall backwards pushing him in offering herself.

Lord Ignacius felt he was shocked by how quickly she was massaging him. It was never so easy to let himself into a woman, easily having no problems.

He just knocked and her doors opened to him all new experience.

He ejaculates quickly in her and he forgot his spandex gloves.

Lord Ignacius let it leak out twice in her how she had her lips taste it from her finger nails in red.

"It was quick."

Simon Says place his hand over his shoulder. "You had your time, let's go back and play those good video games."

"It reminds me of a story about two Tokyo Murray's, moustache and an expensive watch."

"Yes, Ugis Tako loves his Movember style cuts. But I am not sure what it has to do with the Tokyo timeline?"

Captain Mage replies. " You do not worry. When I was in another mission."

.

"There is a honourable reason to extend and drop huge shit bomb in this masterpiece to war criminals due to personal life devastating reasons."

"I hate these Korean inflatable dolls." Lord Ignacius spoke with Sakura Uto on their first unusual date.

"I just cannot understand what our Captain said back then when we left the hotel's carpark."

"Let's never mind and have more coffee. It is our first time; we do not have problems and have time off."

Simon Says interrupts them from a table near them.

"We should join the Korean Police Academy and fock these whores open to our hearts content."

"We should finish the mission first."

"Roger that Captain Mage."

"I am not Korean, I would not fit in."

"Do not worry there will be plenty of women for Lord Ignacius' dreams to come true."

"I am not here for him. I am here to secure a target."

"Simon, you speak a lot. Let's concentrate on map orientacion before we do anything foolish."

"You should have all you can eat while you are in this academy. I heard they have the best seafood."

"I told you Simon Says not to intimidate Lord Ignacius. We are an elite NATO unit and not porn stars. We make living from killing not policing and sexual desires of Korean woman who want policing."

"Yeh but I can feel, they need help."

"Yeh I clearly remember you brought me these Korean cheerleaders in Kansai."

"You were in Kansai?"

"It was another story. Let's focus on our goals."

"Yes Captain and those women did need to sober up."

"We can capture three entry points here and resolve the transit issue on the map but timing is the essence before we establish further contact points."

"How about transporting him out?"

"Don't worry, I have it covered."

"But no cheerleaders this time." Our Captain Mage smiles for the first time.

"Let's give them some metal."

"I think this time you fill inflatable dolls."

.

"You know Karateka Karatedo attack is great defence."

"Yes, an attack in attack."

"Your sensei can punch Joe Senpai?"

"I hit without warning because I cannot care like in a bedroom I handle women."

"Are you in a relationship?"

"I am a free bird who flies high above the skies."

He was looking at her huge Korean chest behind bar stool drinking with her a beer that fateful night before they left to finish the job.

"What an interesting name. What do you do for a living?"

"I am an international truck driver for Tamagochi Freight company."

"I am an office worker. We have lots of pencils on paper to push."

"I think I have a friend who would love it. He is a real office enthusiast."

"His name is Romeo. He can be hiding under the table."

"You are so funny." She laughs concealing her smile under her hand and hugs him.

"You calm down girl. I am engaged to one hot Japanese chick."

"I cannot see your wedding ring. I want you to sing with me in a Karaoke house not far from an overcrowded bar."

"Surely I will show you a great time. I am free tonight. You place good thoughts in my head. I am running a busy schedule tomorrow and we can help each other."

They left in a clubhouse singing and dancing before Simon found her taxi and threw her number on paper in the bin container.

"It is shameful I will not need it because I am taking the first flight home after tomorrow. I think maybe someone else will get lucky with her or our Mage will have me broken apart how I would break her."

Simon said nothing about himself. He just was in a moment he felt was good to find foreign company and relax a little to find himself.

^.^

Their rescue and ambush assault team along the motorway and in the mountain hut. Our unit assembles points to slaughter and secure their target.

"You look at the Korean moon."

"Pfuu." You can hear Lord Ignacius spat on the floor before he spoke over his radio.

Simon Says interrupts Lord Ignacius radio transmission offering a suggestion in his behavior.

"You should not spit indoors."

"I thought you told me to play video games."

"You play with them well."

The organized crime gang convoy was approaching.

"Roger that Live Wire."

Flare Gun

"Are you an artist, Lord Ignacius?"

"I am cubism expressionist creating impression."

"I love your t-shirt but how will you make us look great?"

Lord Ignacius designs made from famous people's faces in cubes collage patterned surveillance cameras' distraction to make it focus to face control to detect his artwork rather than wearing masks.

"It should be a great addition to our laser printer firearms we got in dark web."

"I know they banned blueprints in the US but you are a great video games master."

"Simon, I am working on it. I am not sure how long it will take nor the accuracy of our distractions."

"I know you can handle it, my man. Let's shower after it. I heard Sakura was washing herself."

It is a fatal pivotal point for our heroes to capture their hostage to bring back home before they experience black rain.

"How do you make Tokyo Murray's firearms for us?"

"You ask too much like a cop?"

"I was, but I want to make sure before I lay waste to those War criminals escort to know I fire it."

"It is simple. I send files to a 3D printer from plastic wax and it will build us Lego details. We can assemble it. When we finish it, we can melt it back together and print those lovely collectable dolls."

"How about the bullet velocity of gunpowder?"

"I will use our chemical X to slam those hammers without traceable high velocity piercing power ends to make sure their flag vests will be a significant target."

"Lord Ignacius, I love you my man."

"I know I am the best not only making those sushi cuts."

"Thank you Lord Ignacius."

"I think we are ready to operate Adam Young. I will let Mage know about our trivial matters before we progress our mission."

"You soon join Sakura's shower senses of flowery shampoo. I know you love it."

.

Simon brings in leather vests to show his teammates.

"Sick Sons of Charles."

Lord Ignacius felt surprised viewing gang members' outfits.

"What the fock is this now? I thought I would play video games all weekend."

"We are out for a last ride. We need to let the steam out on the highway."

"Our Mage knows the schedule is a few days later. He said I can choose the time of planning."

"I thought we were about to go home after we can see palm trees once more."

"Nope, and I thought about it, drinking all last night with a Korean doll."

"Ok but how about transport?"

"No worries, I have delightful rides and one pink vest for Sakura."

"Is our Mage now MC?"

"No, he is our Motorcycle Club Captain of Sick Sons of Charles."

Sakura walks in holding back on her shoulders a big bag. "I got us Bersachi illegal helmets."

Lord Ignacius' jaw felt dropped to the floor, thinking today he will ride.

"Yaaaa, is all I can say, arigato Sakura Uto."

They embroidered underneath Seoul.

O.o

The night before they left on their motorcycles, they played strip poker.

Our drunk Simon Says went all in, forcing the Lord Ignacius team to strip off naked before Captain Mage team.

Sakura was watching how they took a selfie photograph.

"Kawaii."

"Yeh we are an evil company."

"We are going wild like no NATO unit."

Captain crossed his hands and shook his head, watching them.

"I told Simon no poker games and now I can see why."

"You know me better like no other brother."

"Ok, let's sober up in the morning before we ride our choppers to a good cuisine stop."

"Ok big boss, you know I am a chef. I can cook it."

"Yes, you were cooking your balls a minute ago on Simon's lap."

"I know it was show off before Sakura."

"I know she left."

"Simon, you can see her because I feel triple Mage in my eyesight. Maybe she is hiding behind a real one."

"I do not think so because I can see a storm in an ocean swaying my boat to the sides."

"Ok, you guys take it easy. I must sleep too."

Their Captain Mage left their hotel room thinking it was good to relax and have fun with school friends he knew long ago, but they never knew him.

It was a perfect past two years for them to learn about him while they trained and fought for NATO units to solve disputes.

It was a great temptation to build unity, acknowledging each other to a deeper unseen seen self.

The perfect human nature is imperfect with our dreaming. Letting us think we are wrong to live and die.

"I think I am getting on with my Christianity Bushido motto."

Magnum Mage spoke to himself before his eyes closed deeper and deeper to sleep.

"We are wrong to live and we are wrong to die."

^.^

When our heroes met local cafe owner Zaf Cok. They had to deal with him in cooking.

It was a long journey before they made a stop before their last drive together.

It was the famous Pakistan's spiciest specialist restaurant on the outskirts of Seoul.

"I can see a couple of motorcycles enthusiasts have arrived. Welcome to my home. It is a great pleasure to serve you our house specialty."

"I think he talks a lot."

"Ya but you keep quiet our failed noodle chef from Osaka."

"You were in Osaka?"

"I know only Uji flavour." Lord Ignacius rushed his finger in a straight line across the table, answering Sakura's question.

"I would love to tell you one day, but we must look forward to the Zaf Cok meal first."

It was a small roadside meal place for hungry travellers to stay in for the day, enjoy gardens, and have a great time behind the table.

"His cooking is like neo-feudalism telemarketing."

"Is it true Sakura? We can taste the spice puddle on my platter."

"I regret to announce. I love high blood sugar." Lord Ignacius fell in love with a full spoonful of curry.

"It is an addictive generation here."

Simon continues loading his stomach full.

"I am happy we all are here together. We must kill more to earn our living."

"Yes, we are the Sick Son of Charles. You are now our chopper's team captain and our homicidal maniac fictional Littland Group leader after the surreal Jon Gi Sigis."

"I take credit for it but we must save the world."

"Mage, I think this curry just saved my day."

"I am happy to eat so much after we stopped those war criminals from killing us."

"I know Lord Ignacius how you stopped them."

"Mage know, and it felt great. I wonder how she is?"

"I hope you left her breathing not like the last one before the last mission you took in?"

Sakura lets her arm sit on Ignacius' lap. "What was your mission in Osaka?"

"It was nothing."

"We just had a great time. We took a business class flight back home and we are here." Simon Says stopped them starting a conversation.

"Let's finish you guys and get in our choppers. I love to have more spins uphill before we start Adam Young."

"Roger that Captain." Simon Says continues to fill in his cheeks full with a hot meal, not letting his eyes off the prize to succeed the empty platter.

When the time came, they took off. Magnum Mage thanked Zaf Cok for his hospitality, shaking his hand and shoulder a goodbye like they knew each other for a long time. "Does he know him?"

"No, but it was a splendid meal." Simon, looking through the window, replies to Ignacius' question.

He takes his Bersachi helmet and starts the chopper, letting everyone in the surrounding area know he started his engine.

They drove off because they started tonight early with the Adam Young project.

.

The NATO legends will never die and will come back to be our heroes.

Magnum Mage's last words before he became a live wire for the operation Adam Young.

It was the central command station codename to be a live wire operator sending coordinate orders to subordinates, helping them complete their field expedition.

"The vehicle is approaching."

"You take the target."

"I'll take it at five."

"How is a torpedo?"

"I have them ready to soften them up."

Simon throws a couple of rocks into a wooden hut.

Three men step out. They are not letting any sounds follow each other's footsteps in the darkness surrounded by a forest.

Simon throws a light flashing torch to a side and murders them along their gunshots fire flashes seeing all three war criminals from Poland drop to a floor.

He walks into a building to secure the perimeter.

"I secured a hostage den and took the chickens inside."

"ok. I have them pissed from the sky, my big bad wolf."

Lord Ignacius was piloting a stolen NATO drone they captured from Polish criminals.

"Their organized crime gang smuggles it in Korea and we're contemplating to sell it for terror."

He opens fire to a first escort vehicle, letting a shower of bullets rain through their transport top.

He was filling them full of bullets holes their dead bodies, taking time to realise he murdered them already.

"I think I just committed a breach of the Geneva Convention in their dead bodies."

"Romeo, do you copy? You stop using other names in our channel and stop killing dead men. You keep aiming and firing at other locations."

"Roger that Live Wire I aim and clear."

He left a carnage the night along the road, allowing the main escort to drive through, taking a turn to emergency contingency plan detour location to meet Simon Says sitting and waiting for them inside.

.

"I remember once a murder case we had in NATO army."

Two single shots murdered Duche Camerita splattering his blood over his family, children and mother.

When synchronised wrist watches beeps at once.

"He was a former politician, but he was a corrupt parliamentarian and leader of the country, causing devastating mass loss to the lives of innocent people."

Magnum Mage spoke before they got ready for a last action.

"It is classified and I will not speak further."

"But you had good pay through PayBitch. I think we all have eye watering accounts through them."

"I am sure you felt great getting rid of this CIA whore?"

"Yes, he was a whore and parliamentarian. I am happy I focked him through a generous NATO donation in PayBitch."

"What do you think about our matching t-shirts tonight?"

"I am not sure about it but we love cash in Japan."

"Teammates, I am happy we done one sick motherfocker splattering pigs blood over his wife and children."

"I wonder not to meet a second sniper because you guys made a risk to your lives."

"Yes, we went under a ghost protocol getting diseased certificates, making them think under fake passports we are in a morgue with a death certificate. It only lasted a couple weeks, and we had him slaughtered in a hurry."

"You just met her. I am Sakura Kawaii from back then. We should be proud of our dates together." Sakura Uto rubs her arm on Lord Ignacius' leg.

"You guys think it is my first time working with Sakura?"

"How he was a whore, parliamentarian and that Cia Cia guy?"

"Simon, we just took our payment in Black Friday Organization."

"You mean supermarket sales in England?"

"It is a sort of sale of rogue agents we find and undertake. You can count us like a funeral home never losing customers."

"It is a funeral house in our club. Simon Senpai does the work for you must first lose your private rank before you can hope for an invitation. You know we are supervising a school field trip."

Lord Ignacius joins his hand under the table with Sakura Uto.

"How about our matching pattern designs for a show I thought we would practice."

Lord Ignacius made a white t-shirt for Magnum Mage to defeat the security camera and become a famous maniac serial killer inside their monitors.

He made Sakura to be found to be Marilyn Monroe. He felt she was a passionate lady he could call his family.

Lord Ignacius designed his looks for surveillance equipment to be Takeshi Kitano, the famous silver screen filmmaker.

Simon Says became Guy Richie's face in the government hide and seek game.

"I know in Korea is a special emergency mobile number. You can dial like 911 to report a spy?"

"It is a strange country. I thought police officers had already had enough prank calls."

"Yes, but they monitor every number in their country. You should dial them if I prepared you to wait for them with a machete."

"I think about it. It is a great tool for a piece of equipment."

Sakura Uto drinks her steel bowl of Soju. "It is the reason I love you, Ignacius-kun. You are never afraid to hit them where it hurts."

"Arigato Sakura and we should be proud of our start to a happy relationship."

"Ok team, I head off to the hotel bed upstairs. I cannot operate our field under influence."

"Sweet dreams, Captain of Sick Sons of Charles. We have a few more steel bowls of milk Soju before we relax."

"We are NATO's secret weapon."

Amadeus Ameterasu

He can hear loud footsteps and loud laughter behind them.

The gun shots were fired from homemade assault rifle clearing Simon Says targets laying waste of three escort bodies.

Two more shots came from outside one body falling in a gun flashlight to a window knocking it break.

Magnum Mage pushed in a thin body covered it's head in black linen bag, his hands tied in plastic rope.

"We are happy we laid to waste polish human smugglers, these narco barons, our war criminals."

"Yes, these pricks were not made withhold European forefathers' minds. I forgot to say I love your laughter."

"I had to distract them."

He takes off his face cover and drops to a pile of dead bodies.

"I left a few leftovers for you outside."

"Yes but now we are in happy hour, shooting and wasting those polished war criminals because they are nothing."

"We will drink Torpedo later."

"This is Live Wire. We have our runaway secure. The streets let your toy back in the barn and wait for us outside with Wildflower."

"I Roger that. The Young Adam operation is over and out."

Simon Says pulls in three more dead bodies with fatal gunshots back to their heads.

"I hate those stinking dead Polish bodies. I hope this house fire will polish them well."

"You make sure ashes to ashes. I will need to attend to our poor hostage to see if he needs any help before we start our convoy back to the north."

Simon Says pulls three more dead bodies to look their dead comrades in the eyes.

"Hey boys make more space because we have our new guests. I forgot to say it is law, every Polish man in my territory licks piss off the floor."

He smacks dead war criminals head to a floor and kicks it's foot, his head, to urine smearing over the floor.

"Yes you like it clean. I know you but retard you are smearing your blood over it!"

When Simon Says completes talking to a dead body.

Mage walks in and asks him to keep it quiet playing his voodoo dolls because the hostage is in possible post traumatic stress disorder and he has no knowledge of Hangul language.

He walks back in a room and cuts off plastic ropes offering a bottle of water.

He checks his pulse to his clock and offer's rice ball wrapped in his napkin from his swiss tactical gear vest.

Simon later drives closer in white van written over it Tamagochi Tools, the best plumbing company in town.

He closes the hostage's head over his arm and walks in through sliding doors closing behind them.

Simon walks out pouring a canister of petrol imitating urine passing through his bowel pouring inside the living room on dead war criminals bodies walking the house laughing and screaming while holding his canister to his waist line.

He strikes a light to his cigarette and walks away blazing a mountain shed in conflagration.

"I nearly fell in love with a blond polish submachine gunner. He was cute. I passed urine on his dead face."

He takes the driver's seat.

"You had to scream so much and laugh, setting this place on fire."

"I think it is great therapy for me and our new friend. It relaxes me."

He is looking at our new friend and smiles blinking one eye as they drive off in Tamagochi Tools transport for the NATO Private Security Unit.

It took not long before they took a stop near a meeting point to collect Sakura with Lord Ignacius. They drove off to a safe house they set to plan to leave the country in a few hours.

"You can call Mark Ta. We have our new friend and we're on our way to Kim Boom Boom."

"We set a secure line in the safe house tower and let them know they will have guests."

"Sakura, you are attending to him. I am not familiar with medical stuff, see his nerve functions with the rest of basic readings before he eats and showers, you keep an eye on with hospitality. Stay close before he rebuilds the basics of normality. It will not be long before we smuggle him out the border."

"Ok, Live Wire senpai."

Sakura places a leather vest of Sick Sons of Charles. He would not feel cold.

The operation was complete. They thought they would escape.

"I will miss Seoul. The Lithuanian Russian propaganda in our homeland is a heavy war machine. They hijack the media spreading misinformation in a disinformation campaign from the Vilnius office that is crippling us."

"I know Simon but we are on the mission and before we head back we have another week under palm trees. We will fly later and listen to our brainwash."

"Yes. I better swap guard and walk in to see how my Sakura Uto is nursing our guy."

"You head in. I know how much you want to work, Lord Ignacius. It is far better to marry her rather than stay in Osaka's noodle kitchen."

"Yes, a speedy noodle delivery."

They both start laughing and swap the night watch.

Lord Ignacius walks in the basement of the house Bibi Bit cousin Ugis Take rented them for the weekend.

"Incheon is great."

He walks in and Sakura is serving tea to the new guy.

"He had not showered yet nor much willing to eat besides Captain Live Wire rice balls."

.

Ramolskis was with brother Jack in Incheon looking for nothing but trouble walking away from their lives.

"I think I saw the other day one guy with a large beard I saved back in the days in Japan when I was backpacking."

"Are you sure?"

"Yes I think I saw him in a police car performing Kansai drift when we were looking off the cliff cafe to a police escort driving away."

"Yes, I think it's destiny to have deja Vu."

"I hope he is doing fine."

"He should be ok. It was long before I licked some possy brother. Let's go out and slap those Korean asses tonight. I have a proper steel boner for them to blacksmith."

"Yes you are Ramolskis looking for nothing but trouble tonight walking away from you is not an option."

"Yes brother Jack, you give me a fist to fist."

"I thought all those years you were locked up in a mental asylum somewhere in England."

"I do not speak to them in English, they never took me in."

"Let's go shooting our love."

"You know how to rock it. Those Korean lovers never win over our seeds in Karaoke."

"I prefer to keep my money, better let's get wasted in the bar. The beer makes girls pretty."

"Yes, let's go shooting those shots."

When they saw police sirens surrounding a house brick fence across the street they joined spectators in a crowd behind a yellow line.

.

They were surrounded with a stolen prosecutor's helicopter on fire planning to run through the demilitarized zone but before the moment they realized they were in the sky.

"It is the police, you are surrounded and leave holding your hands above your hands in peace."

"We are authorized to use live ammunition to stop Littland's Group? Is it true Sergeant?"

"Yes we had approval to seize them and stop them at any price. It was ordered from above, our chief made urgent requests and the prosecutor's office was on it's way with others. They secured us a helicopter."

"We have the whole district police planning to stop their escape routes. They will not get away with human smuggling."

"I see the whole district's police were following Jon Gi Sigis gang footsteps to have them brought to justice."

Simon was looking out the window and counting his bullets.

"I am not confident I have enough gun powder to clear the road out!"

"I had a signal from NATO HQ. We are clear to leave and deliver the package. I think I heard a helicopter is coming for us."

"It is great news."

"Yes but who knows how to pilot it?"

"What do you mean to pilot it?"

Lord Ignacius was placing a flag vest over the hostage's chest and asking him to wear a dark bag over his head.

"I thought we were done having problems!"

"I can."

Sakura Uto volunteered to take the pilot's seat in one last action their team was coordinating.

"We are heading out, load weapons we lay them to waste."

"I whip their heads out."

Simon Says fires a first straight head shot to sergeant's brains splashing blood to his officers faces.

They take cover and draw their handguns out.

Magnum Mage hands out dark medical masks asking to wear them for precaution. They take their CCTV t-shirts.

"Will we wave our white flags?"
"Yes the Streets, your designs are a masterpiece."

Simon nonstop fires at them, filling their vehicles in steel slugs injuring them through weak points hitting them in shoulders, arms and legs leaving them bleeding in a sidewalk.

Magnum Mage walks out first aiming his assault rifle looking for their helicopter.

Sakura and Ignacius follow him, holding between them a hostage, guarding and looking to aim their hand guns to face a flank attack of sides.

They keep their eye gazes aware through a gun aiming mechanism looking for them open.

Simon follows, looking through their backs with an assault rifle.

"Mark one left!"

Simon Says walks away crossing two middle fingers to dead bodies in front of him.

"Die die forces of evil."

"You went too far Simon."

Simon folds his assault rifle to his side. "I was in the force."

Lord Ignacius is laughing.

"I would like to have them in ashes. I could pour them in my ink and tattoo my life tree."

"You focking biders pachinkos! I love blazing those possibilities."

When he is escorting a rescued hostage Magnum Mage asks them to run a detour before more police arrive straight pass an alley along crowds watching them on the street.

"I will have our helicopter ready once you turn around the apartment block."

He walks a faster way to the landing helicopter above the car parking site.

He shoots first round out the window killing the pilot and when he steps in pulling the dead body out his seat he does not notice a prosecutor was in a back seat.

They struggle in the fight to force Magnum Mage to lose his handgun in his right arm once he steps in and fires two shots above the engine.

He fires a left arm assault rifle filling the prosecutor full of cartridge rounds killing him over the blood stained back seat causing the helicopter to smoke.

Simon runs first to him pointing his gun to the helicopter surrounding the front windows to see if his captain survived a gunfire.

"Let's go home, Lithuania!"

Magnum Mage shouts and waves his friends join a smoking helicopter leaving across the border.

Simon waves the remaining tactical team clear to leave behind the wall and board their helicopter.

A Pabluda

Simon straps his seat belt. Sakura sets helicopter altitude to raise the engine wings to take off the ground.

"We are sitting by the fire Simon Senpai?!"

"It is only to keep you hot, sensei."

"I think it is to set our hearts on fire after a secret mission going back to Thailand."

"Let's shout out to all the good times crew and see where the wind blows us."

"Ok."

"I am just not happy to see our poor hostage we must bring back to the North is not feeling well."

"Yes he had enough of those Polish War criminals to kidnap him, planning to smuggle him and sell his organs."

"I always feel the best when I finish my cigarette butt in the dead Polish eye."

"Ok Sakura, set us to the sky."

The propeller wings are blowing black smoke to the sides, taking Seoul Chief prosecutor's helicopter off the ground. Sakura has complex wing control already losing power to the altitude.

Magnum Mage kicks a dead office suit body off his helicopter.

"I am sorry we do not need you here. You are here to soil our seats. Thank you for the ride."

They tilt their nose forward, setting coordinates across the border, but they forgot about dangers awaiting in the demilitarized zone.

When the helicopter was on fire Simon Says heard a radio signal in Hangul.

"We are asking you to turn around. You are in an unauthorized flight across military airspace."

"I am not your brother."

"You have 5 minutes before we stop warning your flight path to correct its destination."

Simon drops his headpieces and shouts to his teammates.

"Fock this Hangul, I never learned it in school. Sakura, you pass the flight control to Captain Magnum Mage."

"What happened?!"

"I cannot hear a thing in loud cabin noise!?"

"Let's grab flare guns and prepare to roll the dice like we are in Macau."

They open both sides of helicopter doors and point their emergency flare pistols waiting for ground earth missiles sounds approaching heat seeking their prosecutor's helicopter on fire streaming black smoke across Korean Peninsula skies.

Our heroes covered the sky in black clouds. They were on a journey.

***

When Simon left the police prison cell. He sat on a chair. He took his back to pure naked skin, showing his muscles.

His memories took him back thinking about the moment it was hard to forget.

He thought to himself in that airplane.

Simon was thinking if his fellow officers sold him they could profit from him in prison but the moment he left it was a bright sky.

The naked back was pure muscle shaped in pulling up his body.

The training before his time would pass for punishment for the crime he never did was great.

The room he sat had windows pointing south allowing most afternoon sun to come in through the window letting in a fresh air breeze.

"You bring me tea, and I have these demon tattoos on my back raising hell."

He was looking for his mobile phone, knowing the time it was.
It was a text message he was sending to a lonely woman he was eager to meet.

A woman from Belarus feltl joy later she learned he was free from steel bars covering his fists.

"I am on my way to your home in Birzu street."
He wrote, thinking to himself.

"I love this asylum whore hiding in a mist of city workers."

He saved her number in his mobile screen contact written MILF.

He drank his tea and rubbed his crotch for sitting too long on the stool, feeling hungry as he left to have his late meal.

He rang a doorbell in a historical building and gates opened, leading him across the court to inner stairs.

Simon walks a couple more steps to the second floor corner flat, feeling his back itching and warm sunlight in the hot summer breeze.

She was waiting for him, smoking cigarettes near the kitchen window, looking outside in a half open satin dress. The colour was red, and she had nothing underneath.

He came closer to see the doors open, and the smell of fresh coffee made him walk in.

Simon walks in and smiles with a tired smile. After those years, he never heard from her.

"It was long before I saw you smoking like that."

It was a romance affair at midday.

"You know our politics. It is a pile of shit. I just want you to love me."

"I love you now."

He lifts her off the chair, sitting her on the lunch table, letting her butt cheeks sit on it.

He spreads her legs to see her, not letting her finish her cigarette.

"I can see you look great. I love you the way you are."

He rubs two wet fingers under her.
She looks him in the eye. He smiles with his gold teeth.

She rubs his bald head. "Your head is bald like you're thinking, Simon. I will take you today."

She pulls him on his black belt, willing to open his blue jeans. Her hand came across his oriental shirt, feeling his hard chest.

He seizes initiative and twists her round and takes her dress up.

They both look at each other in image, outside reflection, looking out at Birzu street, watching how passersby are walking.

He slides his hand closer to her breast, her nipples spreading tighter between his fingers.

He slides in her back to her sides and they look outside together.

She pushes her naked body closer to his black leather belt.

He helps her slide him lower to help him inside her.

"I like it slow."

He can feel her chest breathing, her love beating inside her.

Her cigarette burning makes her inhale another smoke filling her lungs up, exhaling in the air of tobacco and coffee smell.

He completes his mission, tilting Belarusian refugee's hair.

It was years before he was away in a cold cell.

Police officers' prison did not make him any different.

His back is feeling better after five hours of needle work. He stretched a little outside her.

She was pulling him in willing for more of him in her.

Simon knew it would be a story to remember one day to tell.

He stands up, pulling out his love, letting her shoulders relax and her legs stand straight from him.

She wants him a little more than before when checks lower herself to see if he is coming out, looks behind to see him naked.

It felt intense, the breathing the moment she walked to her bedroom door and opened up, letting him follow her.

He did not refuse her.

.

When Simon day dreaming did stop from a moment they made a joke about sex.

He knew before they completed the flight they will start a mission in hell.

"Yes, I know you guys agree about something to joke with."

"I understand after our trauma we should refocus to trace and find illegal weapons dealers."

"Simon, you know I can trust you."

"I find and toast them like no others. You know we are Northern European mind games."

"I hope I will get these noodles toasted for them like we did in Osaka and no Bank of Hokkaido will send killers to look for us."

"We talk well about our sponsors later when we clear our mission and propose my two school friends' proposal to Black Friday organisation."

"I just hate war sponsors. We have to skydive on fire and run away like we are the criminals here."

"The organization is powerful enough to keep us paid."

The massacre and craze horror in the Seoul war operation runs memories to discover the situation about Adam Young project.

"We provide safe extraction once the package is secure and we are heading home."

But they had the face of adversity from corruption in the peninsula, sustaining truth in lies.

Two school friends felt weakness from combat operations in themselves to find hope they could continue to kill and earn their living.

The deployment and briefing was not on the way to Thailand, from where the group took a commercial flight with new allies to the place of the unknown.

They left the hospital and we're transported in military escort to the nearest NATO island on the shores of Japan.

They had been waiting for the brave trio and prepared them fast-track tickets out back on a mission.

Since the potential leak, the commander Mark Ta had no choice but to act in the face of danger to send his teammates and prevent another outbreak of violence on European soil.

Mark Ta had wished them he was in his thoughts with them.

"I think gunfire gives a brilliant light in those dark moments."

"Welcome to the stick man project."

The commanding officer salutes his Chief Commander.

"At ease, soldiers."

Lord Ignacius hands are shaking from combat experience and physical body exhaustion in multiple injuries.

"I hate those local Lithuanian government whores always shielding behind their always per se."

"What are you talking about Lord Ignacius?"

"I think I lost my mind."

"Ignacius had the most damage in the medical report, sir."

"I know the commander but our NATO mission is to assassinate."

"He has a post-combat stress problem."

Mark Ta takes a close look looking in Lord Ignacius eyes to see how he responds to him.

"We all know you are here because your captain sent a distress signal."

"Yes, we work under the covers of darkness imitating criminals."

"You know our silent captain from our school made them pay for it."

"I think we had a violent mission to prevent nuclear winter."

"You are wrong, private."

"What?!"

Mark Ta knew his officer was not in great shape but he was satisfied he was breathing and standing straight to the next flight.

"I learned Simon lost his job in a fake bribery case because they would fill their pockets and leave evidence to set him up like bait."

"Then what?"

Simon iris took a closer look at his NATO Chief Commander.

"I learned from the local team in command, corruption is above the law in the case of a lack of evidence. I sent couple commandos to murder them in their sleeps in robbery case gone south."

"I think it was a clever idea, but I am sad my country rejected me."

"They made me be a noodle chef in a foreign country, only earning enough to afford the same noodles back from my paycheck."

"I think there is no one to blame for this."

"We will talk about it later. We have to focus our planning and see the files before NATO SS Spartacus will land in Salzburg coordinates."

Chief made a solute they left thinking they made a great team in black site from nothing but a couple criminals on the run from law.

He sent a rapport to their Captain Mage to have Lord Ignacius under closer surveillance monitor his mind to avoid pitfalls in the next field operation.

***

Therefore, the elite squad left for an important task.

They found in envelope couple Latvian passports and UN detective licenses issued for 55CIIA agency.

"Great! We are Latvians now."

"How long before we have our access code names?"

"I will have them ready on the ground."

Our heroes, yet with no codenames, left for their mission talkative and taking time to recharge.

"I never supported bidding in pachinko missions but we are on another flight."

"I miss our Tamagochi Tools."

"I know you forgot about our SS Spartacus."

"I am never afraid of work and it is our right to kill."

"I think they have more rights in parliaments than us."

"Yes, our unit regrets to announce that you can get rid of the white collar Hausen Fricken Satanic Pachinko."

"I know Captain, it is white lie you tell us from the day we met in school."

"No, we are sending them to the Polish paradise in dead eye balls."

"You stop joking, my ribs are in pain from the last disaster."

"You think so, it is enough of a joke about our paycheck."

"We must find the source."

"We got that captain Mage."

"I love to fuck when I am back. I love those Russian refugee girls."

"Yes, the runaways from home speak for themselves."

"You only choose peach or cherry filling."

"Lord Ignacius, you know our Lithuanian telepathic propaganda in Russian."
"It must be our telemarketing neo feudalism."

"Yes, we are sex slaves of information disinformation."

"We are like psychics but much better with our Moby Dicks out."

"We know only where to stick our stick when our Lithuanian TV tells us, fuck those refugees, they are lonely."

"I told you we speak from problems, we have to fock perspective."

"What do you want us to do about these girls?"

"Let's focus, we have a mission plan."

"You know better than us."

"I know we were in a coma the whole week and we are asylum hospital look-alikes."

"You can refocus back on the mission plan."

"You love this little misinformation."

"I love to play my FIFA when I'm home."

"You love you to work and kill to earn your living."

"I will continue to dream about our palm trees in Thailand we changed flight plans from."

Simon closed his eyes and took a break before the team briefing started he felt relaxed.

"It is not my fault they hit our helicopter with a ground earth heat-seeking missile when our engine was on fire."

"Yes Magnum, a week in a Korean nurse's hospital was a great way to recover."

Simon was hearing his teammates speak and he was unable to sleep.

"We have a new muscle waiting for us at the checkpoint. His name is Pioter Blat. He is a skilled spy from negotiating espionage to assassinations."

"You think he will be a great asset to our team."
"I think he just finished taping some sort of presidential office depravities. He will lead an intelligence operation on our side. I have a hunch he can discover the weapon's dealership origin."

"What type of parasites are we talking about?"

"We have privateers arming the highest bidders to pay them to make biological warfare weapons to cause mass hysteria."

"What type of weapon is it?"

"It is mass destruction."

"I know mass hysteria is a single delusional belief in large groups."

"Lord Ignacius, I am not talking about dark mind social psychology manipulation."

"I am considering a chemical attack to cause a virus."

"I want to go back to Thailand."

"Lord Ignacius, stay calm if we stop it. We will visit our white sand beaches as many times as we like."

"Why do they pay for it?"

"It is a specific organisation targeting a market selling competitors' economies. I am not a scientist, and I am ordered to trace and murder them."

"I agree with you. We should murder those parasites before their wishful eggs will hatch."

"We have checks to see in the Prague military warehouse. We continue further checks in Vienna, in case we are slow with our sniffer dog, Pioter Blat."

"I hope he will find and cut their throats out. It is what low rented cut throats are for."

"We must complete our NATO project before we become a single crippled stick man from those infections we will find."

"I love Pioter Blat. I think he will poison them with their own shat before they will know about it."

"We are here to do our jobs. I think with Simon's skills, we will have him filling in with slugs before Pioter Blat will know about it."

"No."

"I knew you were not asleep."

He lifts one eyelid to look at them.

"Let's go through data analysis before we will land in five more hours."

"I miss Sakura."

"I will give you her dojo number and later you will contact her family."

"We are like in exams."

"The first question establishes the examiner's intentions, therefore never enter like a belief you knew before you had a question about my dojo of thought."

"I will give you an exam."

"What exam Lord Ignacius?"

"There were hippies. They got eaten by satanists and they converted to police."

"Shut up or I will convert you, too."

"I have great news, your application is in process for Black Friday."

Legal Notice

It's an art of fiction never intended to be a resemblance of living but create an alternative reality parallel to our lives, helping us experience a sensation and entertainment of non-existing events.

If the coincidental information about fictitious forms of work comes into mind, they never intended it to mention neither living nor dead from reality.

About Author

Audrius Razma was born in Lithuania post-soviet era, he finished school in England. He is half blooded Swedish-German and Lithuanian-Latvian.

He admires masters filmmakers Takeshi Kitano and Guy Richie. His research and analysis was learned from a design of a book to be found easily enjoyed like a silver screen movie ticket.

Audrius studied art and design from minimalism design masters, was working in a fine art gallery and travelled the world. He is a writer. Our writer is part of the American Cartel Writers group and professional writers partner in crime.

He has been an author for four years and celebrates the day he started his second birthday on the first of September. His first time ever he started school, picked up his pen and published his first book.

He is now a Business Masters Postgraduate from Spanish Royal Business School, Students Council President and Hiroshima Office Press Editor-in-Chief.

His last book he wrote was acknowledgement and dedication he placed a crucifix in a military drama sequel for him never to be forgotten the day his first child died from Oxford University coronavirus vaccine.

Audrius Razma served in the Army and has a silver Crucifix Award from Pope Franciscus in a diplomatic post for his work.

The word "Sensei" or a Master can mean to be a doctor, teacher or author in Japan.

He believes in the Japanese Communist Party. He writes Christianity Bushido content.

The Hiroshima Office Press.